OUR TEACHER is A VAMPIRE AND OTHER (NOT) TRUE STORIES

BY MARY AMATO

ILLUSTRATED BY ETHAN LONG

HOLIDAY HOUSE / NEW YORK

Greetings, Fellow Classmates,

Our teacher has a huge, frightening secret. I am going to write the story about it in this blank book, and everybody in this class can read it! But first you all have to promise not to tell anybody else. Read the oath below and sign it. At recess, we can each add a drop of our blood to seal the deal.

Suspensefully yours,
Alexander H. Gory, Jr.

P.S. Pass it on, but wait until Mrs. Penrose is not looking.

OaTH

* * *

I agree that this is a Top Secret Book for
Mrs. Penrose's Class <u>Only.</u> Whatever Alexander H.
Gory, Jr., tells me I hereby promise to guard with
my life and never tell a soul. Signed (with a drop
of blood) on this Tuesday, October 22nd, at Delite
Elementary School in Delite, Minnesota.

Sign here _____

Blood here _____

Sign here _____

Blood here _____

Sign here _____

Blood here _____

Sign here _____

Blood here _____

Sign here _____

Blood here _____

Sign here _____

Blood here _____

Sign here _____

Blood here _____

Sign here _____

Blood here _____

Sign here _____

Blood here _____

To Alexander:

1. You are asking us to keep a secret, but sometimes secrets can be bad or even dangerous.

2. I will not pass this book on.

3. We should be listening to Mrs. Penrose's lesson on similes and metaphors. My attention is drawn to her like a magnet.

Sincerely,
Omar

P.S. Just tell me what's going on at recess.

P.P.S. Isn't this the book you got for your birthday to fill up? I like how the pages are perfectly clean and blank. It feels like a real book, not like a notebook.

Fellow Classmates,

This cannot wait until recess. This is a matter of life and death.

Suspensefully yours,
Alexander H. Gory, Jr.

P.S. Pass it on!

P.P.S. Yes, this was a birthday present. I've been saving it for something big, and this is huge!

Hey,

I saw this on ~~Omars~~ Omar's desk and grabbed it. I'm hooked. I promise. But making us wait ~~til~~ till recess is mean. Tell the secret ~~rite~~ right now, Alexander. If ~~its~~ it's as good as you say, I'll pass the book on.

—Carly

Greetings, Carly,

Like I said, the secret is huge. Okay, okay, I'll tell you. Mrs. Penrose is a vampire! You'll never guess who her victim is going to be . . . our librarian, Ms. Yang. I think we'll be the first students to have a vampire for a teacher. My idea is to write the whole story as it happens in this book.

Excitedly yours,
Alexander H. Gory, Jr.

Hey Alexander,

Wow! This is ~~ritly~~ really big news. If we write this story, we could sell it for a ~~millyon~~ million dollars. You could do it yourself. But think about it. With our help, you could do it faster AND it would be more fun AND we would make enough money for everybody to have a lot. I can see this as a movie. You need me!

Later,
Carly

Greetings, Carly,

I like your enthusiasm. Okay. Whoever in the class wants to help write the story can help.

— Alexander H. Gory, Jr.

P.S. Pass it on . . . or else!

Sup, Dudes?

Carly passed me Alexander's book. I'm in. Totally cool idea about the story. Carly's right. We could make big bucks. I'll put in the funny stuff. Alexander can draw the pictures.

By the way, if I were a vampire, I'd pick a nice chubby chap for my victim. Ms. Yang is too skinny. Skinny people like her don't have as much blood as chubby chaps. It's basically like the difference between getting a small soda or getting a Big Gulp. Sluuuuurp!

Smell ya later,
Nick the Slick

Disgusting, Nick. What's your proof, Alexander? Last month you said there was a ghost in the library and there wasn't one.

— Kristen

P.S. I saw a blank book like this at the bookstore and wanted it, but I didn't have any money. Thank you for letting us write in it, Alexander. I'm sort of nervous and excited about how real it is.

P.P.S. You wrote "Pass it on . . . or else." Or else what?

Greetings,

I have all the evidence this time in black and
white. When Mrs. Penrose was helping Buzz in
the back of the room, I went up to her desk to get
a tissue. I saw her journal open and I couldn't help
reading the page.

Meet me under the pine tree by the old merry-
go-round at recess. I'll tell you exactly what I read.

Breathlessly,
Alexander H. Gory, Jr.

P.S. Pass it on or else I will come back as an angry
ghost and haunt you after I die for the rest of your
life.

To Alexander:

1. I can't believe you read Mrs. Penrose's journal. A journal is a private thing. That is completely against the rules.
2. Please stop doing criminal-type things.
3. Mrs. Penrose is way too nice to be a vampire, even if vampires did exist. She is the best teacher I've ever had.
4. A teacher would never bite a librarian, because that is definitely against the rules.
5. I am not passing this book. I do not want to get in trouble. I really wish I didn't sit next to you.

Sincerely,
Omar

P.S. I had to correct the mistakes in Carly's writing because it bothers me to see mistakes.

Excitement at Delite Elementary School

Written by Kristin

At recess, Alexander got me, Omar, Nick, Carly, Jazmine, Tee and Isabella. We all hurried down to the old merry-go-round by the pine tree. The only people from our class who didn't come were Buzz and Harrison. Buzz was too busy playing soccer on the blacktop, and nobody asked Harrison because he's always reading.

The sky was as gray as old metal, and all the trees looked dark and drippy from the morning rain. We sat on the merry-go-round, facing in, because the ground was too wet to sit on.

Alexander held the book out, open to his Oath page. "This is going to be a secret book. Promise not to tell and sign here with a drop of your blood."

"Knock it off, Alexander," I said. "We're not signing anything in blood."

"No blood. No way," Isabella said.

"I promise not to tell," Jazmine said. "Does everybody else promise?"

We did—even Omar, who's afraid of trouble. Alexander was too excited to argue. He took a breath and raised his eyebrows to look dramatic. Then he said in his usual spooky voice, "Our favorite teacher needs the blood of humans to survive. She's a vampire. I saw the proof in her journal."

"The one she keeps on her desk?" Tee asked. "That's her private journal."

"That's what I said," Omar added.

"It was open and he couldn't help seeing it!" Carly said. "Let's move on. We've got a vampire here, people!"

Alexander leaned in. "Here's what she wrote: 'I don't know how much longer I can keep this a secret. No ordinary food tastes good to me anymore.'"

"That doesn't prove anything," I said.

"There's more," Alexander said. "She wrote that she's craving only one thing and said it's the one thing that has always repulsed her. And—"

"What does 'repulse' mean?" Jazmine asked.

Omar spoke up. "Things that repulse you are horrible things that make you sick to your stomach such as drinking human blood—"

"Exactly!" Alexander said.

"And breaking school rules," Omar added, and shot a look at Alexander.

Alexander kept going. "Then she said that she's growing weak and she can't hold out much longer. 'Poor Nou,' she wrote, 'but what else can I do?'"

"Who's Nou?" Jazmine asked.

"Ms. Yang! Our librarian!" Alexander thinks everyone on the planet should know our librarian's first name. "If you guys would stop interrupting me, you'd understand how it all fits together. Number one, she has a secret. Two, she doesn't like ordinary food." He counted off with his fingers. "Three, she's craving something that repulses her, like human blood. Four, she's growing weak. Five, she feels sorry for Ms. Yang—"

"Why would Mrs. Penrose feel sorry for her?" Tee asked. "They're friends."

"Because she's going to sink her fangs into her," Carly said.

"Exactly! Thank you, Carly," Alexander said.

Everybody started talking at the same time, which was creating a muddle of ideas. This was hard, especially for Omar, who doesn't like muddles. We didn't even notice that Nick had disappeared. Suddenly, Nick jumped out from behind the pine tree and lunged at Isabella. He had his teeth stuck out like vampire fangs and said, "Mwa-ha-ha! I vant to drink your blood!"

Isabella started screaming and running, and that didn't help either.

Whew! My fingers just got a lot of exercise. Recess is over. Got to go. It's crazy around here.

To the Whole Class:

1. We have more than one problem.

2. I am making a graphic organizer to help us. At recess tomorrow, please fill it out. I think Harrison and Buzz should fill it out, too, because we are all in this together.

> Sincerely,
> Omar

This is not my fault! Isabella bumped into me, and the book fell in the mud. It isn't her fault either, because Nick was chasing her. It's Nick's fault! Nick needs to apologize to everybody for messing up the book.

Nick's Apology Poem

Add rain to dirt
And you get muddy.
Smear it on the page!
Who thinks it's cruddy?
Only one big fuddy-duddy.

Nick, your poem was not an apology. I don't like mud either. Let's all be more careful! This is a very nice book! :)

— JAzmine

Name:	Is Mrs. Penrose a vampire? (yes or no)
Omar:	No
Alexander:	Without a shadow of a doubt
Carly:	Let's all say she is.
Nick:	Absolutely
Tee:	I don't think so. But if she got turned into one I feel bad for her because I'm sure she doesn't want to be one.
Kristin:	Would need more proof.
Jazmine:	If she is, we'll cure her.
Isabella:	No. Vampires ~~is~~ are bad people.
Buzz:	Stop bothering me. I'm in the middle of a game.

Should we keep writing about it in this secret book?
(yes or no)

No

Yes

Yes! $$$$$$$Cha-ching!

Abso-dabbo-lutely

Yes, because I want to be a writer,
only I never have ideas.

Yes, as long as it is a realistic story.

Yes. We could add glitter and those
nice-smelling scratch stickers
to make it fun. No more mud!

No. This will make trouble.

No. Why would anyone want to write
unless you had to?

To Write or Not to Write

by Kristin

It is official! We will keep writing in this book. We had another meeting at recess today. Six people voted yes. Three people voted no. Harrison didn't vote because nobody asked him. I wanted to ask, but Carly said, "He's busy reading. Let's just go, go, go."

We were all sitting on the old merry-go-round again because the ground was still wet.

As soon as the votes came in, Alexander yelped. He started hopping on and off the platform. "We need to write down everything that happens. Let's follow Mrs. Penrose at midnight to catch her in the act."

Carly was in second place for being hyper. "Vampire books sell, especially if we say that a vampire is running loose." She started jumping on the platform, making the rest of us jiggle. "We can also sell garlic necklaces because garlic keeps vampires from biting you. We can make a fortune."

"If we are telling people Mrs. Penrose is a vampire, they will not let her be a teacher," Isabella said.

"Or she'll come after us," Nick said. "We'll all turn into vampires and get capes and grow fangs and scare the kindergartners. Mwa-ha-ha!" He jumped off the merry-go-round and started spinning us around, which made Isabella scream.

"Knock it off, Nick," I said, but it was kind of funny because Isabella sounds like a flying monkey when she screams.

(No offense, Isabella. You have to admit, it's true.)

"We don't need to say that <u>Mrs. Penrose</u> is a vampire. We could change her name so people who read our book won't know it's her," Alexander said. "Then she wouldn't get fired."

"Perfect," Carly said.

"We can call her Mrs. Pennytoes," Nick said, and laughed.

"Not ghoulish enough," Alexander said.

Omar had been quiet until now. "I voted no because I don't want to get in trouble. But I do like the idea of us all writing a big story together. Why don't we write a novel like Mali Koam's 'The Deep Blue'? That was an excellent book. As long as we do it In our free time, Mrs. Penrose can't get mad at us for that."

"Let's make it about fairies," Jazmine said. "We can make Mrs. Penrose the Queen of the Woodland Fairies."

as if

Alexander let out a big breath. He looked like

he was about to have a hissy fit. "You're missing the point. We're not making up stories here. This is a real thing!" He stomped at the end like an exclamation point. "It's <u>my</u> book and <u>my</u> idea. I'm writing the vampire story by myself. Case closed."

"No takebacks," I reminded him. "You said we can help write the story. You wrote that down in this book. We're all writing one big story together."

"We need Kristin," Carly said. "She's like a reporter. She writes the fastest."

"Okay, okay." Alexander nodded. "But it has to be the vampire story. It's the story of the century, and that's what we voted on anyway." He stared at Omar. "If anybody doesn't want to write with us, that's fine."

Omar looked up at the sky as if the clouds would tell him what to do. "The majority does rule," Omar said. "I can't argue with that. I want to write as long as we don't break rules."

Carly jumped off the merry-go-round and announced: "It's the vampire story, but only at recess or free time. That's a wrap."

(Carly has been saying "that's a wrap" ever since she went to Make-a-Movie Camp, because that's what the director says when a scene is over.)

The bell rang, and we all had to come in for lunch. I just wrote all this with my right hand while eating a peanut butter and bacon sandwich with my left hand. I am adding one thing that I forgot to say.

Carly, I'm sorry but I don't think people will buy garlic necklaces because they will smell bad, but thank you for the compliment about my speedy writing and I do admire your spirit.

Yo Carly,

I disagree with Kristin. Sell garlic shampoo and garlic sandwiches, too. We'll all smell horrible. Ha-ha.

Smell ya later big-time,
Nick the Slick

Greetings,

I know Omar is going to get mad, so don't pass this book to him. But there's exciting news that cannot wait until free time or recess tomorrow. After we came back from lunch, Nick told me that he found more proof.

"Go look in her cup!" he said.

I went up to "get a tissue" and saw inside Mrs. Penrose's white cup. It's not filled with water. It's filled with dark red liquid. Blood!

Seriously yours,
Alexander H. Gory, Jr.

P.S. Pass it on or else toads and locusts will fall on your head like rain.

Hey,

   I just went up and looked. It is blood!!!!!!!!!!!!!!!!

                  great
This will be a ~~grate~~ part of the story.

                              Later,
                              Carly

Dear Alexander,

   I doubt it's blood. I think we should come up with
another story idea to write about. The vampire thing isn't
                        were
realistic. If Mrs. Penrose ~~was~~ a vampire, she'd be sleeping
in her coffin during the day. When sunlight touches
vampires, they burst into flames. Remember when she
took us outside to explore the creek during science last
week? It was sunny. There's the proof. You have to look at
all the evidence.

                              —Kristen

P.S. The only thing different I notice about Mrs. Penrose
is that she's getting . . . well . . . let's just say she has been
sneaking an extra dessert or two at lunchtime, if you
know what I mean.

To the Whole Class:

1. I am mad because we agreed no book during class. I'm only writing in this because I finished brainstorming my predictions for the leaf experiment.
2. I predicted that the leaf that's in the cup of water in the sunlight will stay green.
3. I was going to ignore the book, but then I saw Carly's entry as Kristin was passing the book back to Alexander. I had to correct Carly's mistake. I found mistakes in Kristin's writing, too.
4. I'm informing everyone right now that I will be correcting any and all mistakes that people write in this book. It's like when I practice the piano. My ears hurt if I make a mistake and don't go back and correct it.

Sincerely,
Omar

Deer Omar,

　　Rozes are red.

　　Dirt is dirty.

　　Here are sum misteaks

　　To make your ears hurty.

　　Ha ha ha ha ha ha.

　　　　—Nick

Ha ha ha ha ha NOT.

　　　　— Omar

Greetings, Class,

　　Back to the real subject. Mrs. Penrose. My theory is
that she's a newly bitten vampire. Last week she was an
ordinary human and could experience sunlight on her
skin, but over the weekend she was turned. Now she's
trying to learn how to be a vampire. She's still clinging
to her human ways because she doesn't want to stop
being our teacher. Who would? She's trying to stay
awake during the day and stay out of the light. She's
lucky, because this week it has been gray and rainy.

　　When we catch her in the act, we shall help her
to live as a vampire teacher. We shall keep the shades
down and let her sleep during the day. We shall find
good blood for her to drink. Perhaps we can get it
from the hospital. I think they have cupboards full of it.

Suspensefully yours,
Alexander H. Gory, Jr.

P.S. I can't wait to see Mrs. Penrose drink what's in her
cup. Pass it on!

Hiya Boys and Ghouls,

Why doesn't she take a sip already? I agree with the big A-man. Mrs. Penrose is x̶-̶t̶r̶a̶ extra tired. Did you notice that she fell asleep at her desk this morning? It was hilarious. She was starting to drool. She was probably up all night sharpening her fangs.

Peace out and pass the pancakes,
Nick

Hey,

M̶i̶l̶l̶y̶o̶n̶ Million dollar idea—along with this book, we could invent a fang sharpener and sell it to vampires. BTW, she just yawned. I think she's g̶o̶n̶n̶a̶ going to take a sip soon.

Later,
Carly

Dear Everybody,

This is Isabella. Finally, I get a turn to write.
I love this special book! But it is not blood in the cup!
After lunch, I walk in and see Nick. He pours the water
out of Mrs. Penrose's cup and pours ~~jus~~ juice
into it. The cup is white and the ~~jus~~ juice
is red so it looks like blood!

— Isabella Diaz

She's right! I walked in, too.
"What are you doing, Nick?" I asked.
"A little switcheroo," he said. "Don't
tell anybody. Ha-ha."
Then Mrs. Penrose and all you guys
walked in and class started and we didn't
know what to do. We tried to get this book
and write down the truth. But you guys
were hogging it.
This is bad. We'll get in big trouble
because of Nick.

— Jazmine

Nick, you rat! You got my hopes up and then dashed them. I wanted it to be blood.

— Alexander H. Gory, Jr.

Come on, dude! When you saw it, your eyes almost popped out of your head. That was hilarious. Ha ha ha ha.

— Nick

It won't be funny when Mrs. Penrose drinks it, Nick. Look at it this way. She'll think we're playing a trick on her, and that could hurt her feelings. Vampire or not, she's our favorite teacher. Fess up now, before she takes a sip. We're on the edges of our seats.

— Kristen

The True Story of What Happened Next

by Alexander H. Gory, Jr.

Soon the whole class knew the truth about Nick's little trick, and the suspense was killing us. At first I was mad at Nick, but then I realized it was exciting. Putting punch in the cup of a teacher is one thing. Putting punch in the cup of a vampire is another. Would she get mad? Would anger make her fangs pop out?

"So, how many of you have finished writing down your leaf-experiment predictions?" Mrs. Penrose asked. Then she picked up her cup.

It was like slow motion. We were all holding our breath. While she was still looking at us, she brought the cup to her lips. She was about to take a sip when . . .

Knock, knock!

Surprised, we all turned toward the door.

"Pardon the interruption," Mr. Suarez said. "I was hoping I could borrow your 'Pioneer Days' book for this period, if you're not using it."

"You betcha," Mrs. Penrose said. She set her cup down, got the book and walked over to the door. She and Mr. Suarez stepped out, yack-yacking the way teachers always do.

Then Jazmine surprised everybody. She jumped up and grabbed Mrs. Penrose's cup, dumped the punch into the sink, put the cup back and sat down.

The rest of us were speechless.

Mrs. Penrose walked back in.

"Now, where were we?" she asked, and sauntered to her desk. "Oh yes . . . the predictions . . ." She sat on the edge of her desk, picked up her cup and noticed it was empty. Her forehead wrinkled.

Thump, thump.

Thump, thump.

That was the sound of our racing hearts.

"I thought I had water in here," she said.

"Um . . . with all this time gone by perhaps it evaporated," Omar said.

"Or maybe you already drank it," Jazmine said.

"Or perhaps that ghost Alexander dreamed up last week drank it when you weren't looking," Kristin said.

Mrs. Penrose smiled at that. And then she went on with our lesson as if nothing had happened. No anger. No fangs.

The danger is over, and I must say that I'm disappointed.

But there's always tomorrow. The sun is supposed to come out. We shall try to lure Mrs. Penrose into the light and see if she panics.

Farewell!

Alexander H. Gory, Jr.

The Moment of Truth

by Kristin (during recess)

First of all, let me say that there is nothing like having a secret book and possibly having a vampire for a teacher to make you want to come to school.

This morning when my bus pulled in, Carly was by the front entrance handing out fliers she made.

Garlick Necklaces for Sale

Vampires are lurking everywhere

Order your garlick necklace at recess today

See Carly

Only $1.99

Protection from Vampires guaranteed

Garlick is spelled garlic, but that's not the point.

Jazmine, Tee and Isabella were there, too.

"This is crazy," Isabella whispered. "Everybody is talking about vampires now."

"It's great," Carly said. "I have five orders. I learned from my last mistake. I'm taking your advice this time, Kristin."

(That was nice to hear, because last month Carly got mad at me. She made all those cool friendship wristbands and tried to sell them for five bucks, and I told her to lower her price.)

"Finally, the sun is shining!" Alexander shouted. He was the first off the 214 bus. He came running with the book. "This will be a moment of truth," he whispered.

Nick followed, looking all serious. Then he raised his eyebrows in this creepy way and smiled. He had fangs in his mouth! Isabella screamed, even though they were plastic.

It was time to go in, so he had to put them away.

In our classroom, golden rays of sunlight were streaming in the windows like an old friend coming back to say hello. Unfortunately, Mrs. Penrose was sitting at her desk, which is far from the windows.

"Good morning, class," she called out.

"We have to get her to step into the light," Alexander whispered while everybody said good morning.

Just then Ms. Yang walked in. She was wearing a blue dress with a pretty blue and purple scarf tied around her neck.

Alexander touched my shoulder. "Look," he whispered. I could tell what he was thinking: She's hiding her neck with a scarf because Mrs. Penrose bit her. Let's lure them both over to the window and see if they burst into flames.

"Good morning, class. Good morning, Mrs. Penrose. Here are the books you ordered. And I brought you a little gift. I hope it helps." Ms. Yang gave Mrs. Penrose a stack of books and a box tied with a blue ribbon.

"What a fun surprise," Mrs. Penrose said, and opened the gift. "Oh, thank you so much, Nou. You're a lifesaver."

Curiosity was zipping through our brains. We wanted to know what was in the box.

They hugged, and Ms. Yang left. We had to do the usual lunch orders, pledge, morning meeting, etc. Alexander was jiggling so much his desk kept hitting the back of my chair.

He tapped my shoulder and whispered, "What do you think is in it?"

I shrugged.

"Maybe vials of blood," Alexander whispered. "Or a little pillow for her coffin."

Finally he couldn't stand it anymore. He did this very big fake sneeze, and then he went up to get a tissue. He pretended that he wasn't looking at Ms. Yang's gift, but he did.

His face had a strange expression when he sat down.

I turned around and whispered, "What was in it?"

"Foot lotion, bath oil and tea," he whispered. "I don't get it."

He pulled out this book to write, but then Nick tried to grab it and then Omar said, "Put it away," in a voice that was louder than a whisper.

Mrs. Penrose cleared her throat in that special way that means to hush, and we all got quiet.

"Alexander, could you come up here for a chat and bring that book?" she asked.

Like walking the plank, Alexander went to her desk.

They whispered for a while, and then she sent him back without the book. His face was red.

I was going to write what happened next, but Omar got the idea that it would be better if Mrs. Penrose wrote it down in this book so the truth would be in her own words.

See the next page to find out what she writes!

The Secret Book

by Mrs. Penrose

Something was in the air at Delite Elementary School. For the past several days, my students had seemed distracted and anxious. I thought perhaps it was due to the gloomy weather. Today, though, the sun came out, and yet when my students arrived they seemed more distracted than ever.

After a quick visit from Ms. Yang, I noticed Alexander acting strangely. Then a fight with a book broke out. Curious, I called him up to my desk.

"What is going on with the book, Alexander?" I asked.

"What book?" Alexander asked.

"The one you're holding," I said. "May I have permission to read it?"

"It's just an old thing," he said. "Lots and lots of completely blank pages."

"It's your birthday book, isn't it? I remember when you got it and were wondering what to put in it. I noticed that you've been writing in it now, which is great, but I'm concerned that it's causing a distraction. May I see it?"

"You're probably too busy to read it right now," Alexander said.

"Will I be unhappy to read it?" I asked.

"That depends," Alexander said.

"On . . . ?"

"On how you feel about being a creature of the dark," he said.

Now I was definitely curious. Alexander handed me the book, and I asked him to sit down. While my students sat in silence, I read page after page. Then I closed the book.

"Class," I said, "we have some important things to discuss. First of all, it seems that Alexander read my private journal without my permission and then shared what he read with you. He shouldn't have done that."

"That's what I told him," Omar said.

"I'm sorry," Alexander said quickly.

"He has a hard time controlling himself," Carly added.

"I accept your apology, Alexander," I said. "Second of all, it is not wise to read a vampire's private journal, because when vampires get mad, they bite."

Isabella almost fainted.

"Just kidding," I said quickly. "I'm not a vampire."

Nick laughed. "Good one, Mrs. Penrose."

"I should prove it, though," I said. I pushed up my long sleeves and said, "Drumroll, please."

My students all made a drumroll on their desks.

Slowly, I walked toward the windows. I stepped into the sunlight and . . . I burst into flame!

Just kidding. Nothing happened.

"See?" I said. "I'm not a vampire."

"But what about everything you wrote in your journal?" Alexander asked.

"I do have a secret," I said. "And it's time that I reveal it."

All eyes were on me.

"Actually, it will be more fun if I make you guess." I pulled the foot lotion out of the gift box that Ms. Yang gave me and handed it to Alexander. "Can you please read the brand name of this lotion?"

"Mommy-to-Be Foot Lotion."

I smiled. I turned to the side and put my hands on my belly.

Omar's eyes were the first to light up. "You're going to have a baby!"

I nodded. Jazmine jumped up and hugged me. Tee followed, and everyone clapped.

"When is it coming?" Kristin asked.

"Not until March," I said. "The craving I was writing about in my journal was for burgers, not 'the blood of humans' as Alexander wrote."

"But you're a vegetarian," Jee said.

"I know! That's why it's been a challenge."

"My mom craved steak when she had me," Kristin said.

"What about Ms. Yang?" Omar asked. "Why did you write 'Poor Nou'?"

I smiled. "You all know that she's my friend as well as our librarian. Did you know that she's also a vegetarian and we eat lunch together? She knows about the pregnancy and also knows I've been craving burgers. She jokingly said that she'd be lonely if I started eating meat, so that's why I wrote 'Poor Nou.'"

"And you're tired a lot because it takes a lot of energy to make a baby," Kristin said.

"That's true," I said. "Now, about this book."

The class grew quiet.

"As you know, I love writing," I went on. "But passing around the book during class is not cool. Many of you have been paying more attention to it than to my lessons."

"That's what I told everybody," Omar said.

"We're sorry," Jee said.

"Please don't be mad," Isabella begged.

"You know that I want you to become better writers this year," I said. "And you all seem eager to write in this book. So I'll let you keep the project going—"

The class erupted in applause.

I held up my hand. "As long as you only write in it during free time—that's free time before school starts, after you finish your work, at recess or lunch, or at the end of the day. Agreed?"

Everyone agreed.

"Also please ask classmates if they would like to write in it, even if it seems they would prefer to do something else, such as . . . read, for example."

Everyone agreed.

Happy writing!

To the Whole Class:

1. Mrs. Penrose is human!

2. Mrs. Penrose is having a baby!

3. We get to keep writing in this book!

4. I have an idea for what to write next. Please add your letter of congratulations to Mrs. Penrose below. I have done the first one as an example. Please everybody do it.

Dear Mrs. Penrose,

Thank you for not being mad at us for thinking you might be a vampire. I know you will have a smart, good baby.

Sincerely,
Omar

Hey Mrs. Penrose,

I'm sorry ~~youre~~ **you're** not a vampire because we

~~coulda~~ **could have** made some money off you. But I got

hooked on the idea of us writing a big story and

selling it, so we need to do it in here. AND I'm

excited you're ~~gonna~~ **going to** have a baby.

Later,

Carly

P.S. I hope you have a really cute baby, ~~cuz~~ **because**

then you can take it to Hollywood and get it on

TV. That's my free advice for you.

Greetings,

I am sorry I read your journal and will not do it again. I am also sorry that you are not a vampire, because that was thrilling while it lasted. I do want to write a big scary story with everyone, so thanks for letting us.

You will make a fantastic mother. Tip: Let your kid have some pets. Snakes and tarantulas make perfect ones.

Farewell,
Alexander H. Gory, Jr.

P.S. If your baby turns out to be something exciting like a baby werewolf or an alien, tell us so we can write a story about it.

Hurray! You're having a baby! Hurray! I hope it's a girl! We are so happy!

Cheers,
Jazmine

Teachers love to teach.

Vampires love to slurp.

I hope you have a baby

who really loves to burp.

— *Nick the Quick*

Dear Mrs. Penrose,

Eat whatever you want. My mom says you have to eat like a pig when you're pregnant. I just realized my mom says a lot of similes, and I bet she doesn't even know it. Oh, and she also says extra pounds keep you warmer in the winter, and that's why God invented chocolate cake.

—Kristen

Dear Mrs. Penrose,

You are a teacher with a lot of wonderful ideas. I am so happy that you are my teacher. Your baby will be happy you are her mom when she is born. I can't wait. I asked my mom to have me a baby sister or brother and she said no, which made me sad because I love babies. Now I am so happy because you're going to have one. Can you bring the baby in right away and can we all take a turn to hold her? Or him?

Yours truly,
Tee

Dear Mrs. Penrose,

Please make that baby come when it is spring break. After spring break, please bring that baby here and keep teaching. Then there won't be one day where you are not here when we are here. I dont don't like it when you are not here.

—Isabella

Dear Mrs. Penrose,

"A baby is like a sunrise. Seeing one is just a good way to start every day." That's a quote by Mali Koam from her book "Fur," but you probably know that.

Congratulations (and thanks for letting me borrow that book),

Harrison

P.S. This is my first time writing in this book. I really like it.

Mrs. P.,

I'll teach the lil guy how to be the world's best striker. A striker is the one who gets the goals in soccer, in case you didn't know. Go big or go home!

— Buzz

Dear Boys and Girls,

Sorry that I am an ordinary human.

It was interesting to read all of your good wishes. I am just hoping for a healthy, happy baby. Even though the vampire story didn't turn out to be true, I'm sure you'll find another story idea to write about in this book. By the way, let's keep it on the shelf in the Good Book Nook. That way, you won't be tempted to pass it during class. Remember, as long as everyone is invited to write, and as long as the book doesn't cause any problems, you may keep this cool, collaborative project going.

Your teacher,
Mrs. Penrose

P.S. A "dust jacket" is a paper cover that folds over the front and back covers of a book to protect it. If you want to make a dust jacket for your book, Ms. Yang can show you how.

Hey,

    Good morning. I have HUGE news. I told my mom we were all writing a book, and she showed me a contest. ~~Its~~ It's for any kids between 2nd grade and 5th grade to send in a story. The prize is $100!!!!!!!!!! I'm not so good at writing, but if we did this together we could win. ~~Lets~~ Let's keep the contest a secret so nobody else enters. When we win it will be a big ~~suprize~~ surprise. During recess, ~~lets~~ let's get started. That's a wrap!

                        —Carly

    Hurray! Really fun idea, Carly!!!
    If we win, Mrs. Penrose will be proud of us. I can't wait for recess!

                        —Jazmine

Hi,

I love this, but I do not have any ideas for stories. It is a big problem for me.

Sadly,
Tee

Yo Tee,

Here is a joke to cheer you up.

What did the pen say to the pencil?

Nothing. They can't talk. Ha-ha.

Adios,
Nick

Fellow Classmates,

Our big story should be scary. Halloween is coming. Maybe we should meet in a cemetery at midnight tonight and find a ghost to write a story about.

Farewell,
Alexander H. Gory, Jr.

P.S. Remember, I'm the one who thought of this book idea in the first place.

Dear Everybody,

The cemetery is scary at midnight. My abuelita says they are haunted. There are other ways to get good
                    aren't
ideas that ~~aren't~~ scary.

—Isabella

P.S. We should not get up our hopes about the contest. We might not win.

To the Whole Class:

1. The best way to get ideas is to brainstorm.

2. I will make a graphic organizer at recess.

Sincerely,
Omar

P.S. Besides spelling problems. I've noticed contraction problems, especially with Isabella. "... ideas that <u>arent</u> scary" should be "... ideas that <u>aren't</u> scary" because the sentence is really "... ideas that <u>are not</u> scary." The apostrophe is like a little cutter that cuts out the letter "o" in "not" and makes two words into one.

We all make mistakes. I remember when Isabella came here in Kindergarten she was just speaking Spanish. She's learning fast! My grandmother can't spell or talk English very well even though she has been here a long time, because she grew up in Vietnam.

—Tee

No organizer! Let's just write an amazing story. It will be faster if we just do it. Morning free time is over so see y'all at recess. That's "you" and "all" smooshed together to make "y'all."

— Carly

I don't think "y'all" is a real word, but you've got the idea.

— Omar

Poem for Omar

"Y'all" is real.

So are "ain't" and "sup."

These words are called slang.

Dude, lighten up.

Ha ha ha.
— Nick the Quick

Notes about Recess

by Kristin

Well, recess was as much fun as watching water go down a drain.

Argue. That's all we did. How can we ever write anything if we can't get a good idea that everyone likes?

It's sad, but I think this whole plan to write a story together is officially dead.

Kristin,

You can't just write the word "argue" and put a period after it. That's called a sentence fragment.

— Omar

Give it a rest, Omar! I'm not writing to the President of the United States. Every sentence doesn't have to be complete.

—Kristen

Hey,

I have a big idea to get us going again!!!!!!!!!!!!!!!!!!!!! You'll find out what it is tomorrow, y'all.

—Carly

Carly's Surprise

by Alexander H. Gory, Jr.

Ah, the tingle of suspense. Thanks to Carly, all night long it felt like spiders were crawling under my skin. What was her big idea? When would she reveal it?

She arrived at school with a bag in her hand, and she held it up but she wouldn't let us see what was inside.

"Give us a hint," Jazmine begged.

"It will help us with our story contest," Carly said.

I looked at the size and shape of the bag.

"Is it a mysterious skull of someone who has been murdered?" I guessed.

"No," she said.

"Is it photographic proof of a famous mystery like the Loch Ness Monster?" I guessed.

"Nope," she said.

"Is it a machine to detect ghosts?"

"No," she said, and put it in her cubby. "And that's all I'm saying until recess."

We have to wait. Agony!

Carly's Surprise, Continued

by Kristin

During the morning, Alexander was jiggling like a maniac. Mrs. Penrose noticed right in the middle of a lovely little lesson on alliteration. She walked over and whispered to Alexander. "Hey, buddy boy. You've been distracted this entire period. Is your brain muddled? Do we need to have a Muddle Huddle?"

"Yes," said Omar, even though she wasn't asking him.

"Yes," added Buzz, because he loves Muddle Huddles.

"Time for a Muddle Huddle!" Mrs. Penrose announced.

Harrison looked confused, because he's new this year and didn't have Mrs. Penrose like we did last year. He hasn't done a Muddle Huddle or a Touchdown Twist yet. They're silly things Mrs. Penrose made up, but they work.

We all got into a huddle. Mrs. Penrose whispered to us like a coach. "All right, team. I can tell we're distracted. We need to find our focus. Who can say what we're studying right now?"

Jazmine raised her hand the fastest. "We're studying alliteration."

"Right. Why?"

I shot my hand up. "Slipping words with similar starting sounds into the same sentence can sparkle up our style."

Mrs. Penrose laughed. "Yes! That's an awesome alliterative answer, Kristin. Let's go over it."

We practiced my answer a few times and then we were ready. We all put our hands on top of one another's in the middle like a stack of pancakes. We did this next part with "energy," which means not too loud, not too soft, just right.

Mrs. Penrose called out, "What are we learning about?"

"Alliteration!" we exclaimed.

"Why?"

"Slipping words with similar starting sounds into the same sentence can sparkle up our style," we said.

She laughed again. "When are we doing this?"

"Now!"

Then we made our hands fly up at the same time. Harrison looked freaked out, but you could tell he liked it.

We went back to our seats and had fun writing sentences with alliteration. Like I said, Muddle Huddles are silly, but they work.

Finally recess arrived. We ran down to the merry-go-round. Even Buzz came. Tee remembered what Mrs. Penrose said about making sure everyone was included, and she told Alexander to go back up to the blacktop where Harrison was reading and say "Please come," and he did.

Once we were all there, Carly opened the bag and pulled out a box. "Ta-da!"

"It's just a shoe box," Buzz said.

"It is not," Carly said. She showed it off. It had fake money glued all over it and a slot cut in the lid. It said Carly's Secret Story Contest on the side in big letters. "I'm announcing my own contest. Everybody has to write a great story and then fold it up and put it in this box. I'll read all the stories and pick the best one. It's like a little contest to decide which story should go on to the big contest."

"It's sort of like the qualifying matches in soccer," Buzz said. "The winner goes on to the World Cup."

"Yep," Carly said. "It'll be fun, fun, fun."

"Are you going to read the stories out loud?" Tee asked.

Carly nodded. "At recess tomorrow. I'll pick a winner and help the writer make the story more exciting. Then I'll enter it in the big contest and split the prize money."

Tee's face got sad. "I don't have any ideas for stories. That's my problem."

Carly pulled out a dollar from her pocket and waved it in the air. "This will give you ideas. It's called motivation."

"Is that the prize?" Omar asked.

"Yep," Carly said.

"One dollar? Forget it," Buzz said. He dropped his soccer ball on the ground and dribbled it over to the soccer field.

Carly made a face. "We don't need him anyway. I'm going to put this box in my cubby. Tomorrow morning, everybody put your story in it. Tomorrow at recess, we'll meet here and I'll read all the entries. That's a wrap."

"Who made you the boss? What if I want to write one and send it to the contest myself?" Nick asked.

"That wouldn't be fair," Carly said. "I'm the one who told you about it."

"Are you going to enter your own story?" Omar asked her.

"I'm the judge," Carly said. "Now I'll give you all time to think about your stories."

She walked to the blacktop with her box.

Nick jumped up and said, "Boys and ghouls, that's a wrap!" and then he started chasing after Isabella. She screamed like the most mad, mortified, maniacal monkey in the history of Minnesota.

Greetings,

Another night of sleepless suspense! Who wrote stories for Carly's contest? Which story will win? Will the story be scary enough to satisfy me? Unfortunately Cruel Carly duct-taped the lid on her box so we can't sneak a peek before recess.

Mrs. Penrose just announced that we are starting our lesson on exaggeration and hyperbole, whatever that means. The morning is going to take forever. I have to put this book away even though it is killing me.

— Alexander H. Gory, Jr.

The Secret Story Session

by Kristin

"Drumroll, please," Carly said at recess. We were all on the merry-go-round.

Nick created a loud earthquake with his feet by hopping back and forth on the metal platform really hard.

"Knock it off, Nick," I said. "That's making me sick."

"Your face makes me sick, Krusty," Nick said, and started to laugh his head off.

I didn't get upset, because he isn't being mean. He's just being Nick. Besides, I learned how to handle him in kindergarten. "Thank you, Nickerless," I said. "I'm so happy I can make you sick without even trying."

"Quiet on the set," Carly said. "I'm going to open the box."

We were all curious. Even Buzz and Harrison came without being asked. I thought maybe there wouldn't be any stories at all. I didn't write a story, because I couldn't decide on an idea.

She opened the lid. It was full of folded-up papers.

"Wow," Carly exclaimed. "This is fantastic!"

"Read that one first," Jazmine said, and pointed to one that had hearts on the outside.

Carly opened it up. " 'The Story Writers' by Jazmine."

"Carly, since you get to be the judge," Omar said, "can one of us read the stories?"

"Okay," Carly said, and handed him the paper. "That way I can listen better."

Omar read: "Once upon a time there was a classroom full of nice students at Delite Elementary School. One beautiful day, their wonderful teacher (who is going to have a baby) gave them free time to write a story. A girl named Jazmine got to go first. Happily, Jazmine took out her pen and began to write. Suddenly the students heard a cheerful tune coming through the window. Was it a fairy singing? It was! The fairy turned Jazmine's pen into a glitter pen and gave everybody glitter pens. Everybody was happy. The End."

Alexander couldn't help himself. "What about a werewolf instead of a fairy? What about some blood and guts and scary stuff?"

Jazmine rolled her eyes.

"It was full of imagination and surprises, Jazmine," Tee said quickly.

"It is brave to write," Isabella added. "I am chicken."

"I'll consider it," Carly said. "Let's read the next one." The second paper she pulled out was blank. She made a face and pulled out another. It was blank, too.

"This isn't funny," she said, and Nick started laughing.

"A complete waste of paper," I said.

Carly opened five more and they were all blank. Nick was laughing so hard that Marcos and DeeNice and Lauren from Mr. Suarez's class came, and we had to tell them it was a private meeting. Then finally she opened one with some writing. She handed it to Omar.

"The Secret Box," Omar read.

"Ooooh. I love that title," Carly said.

Omar read on. "Once upon a time, a girl named Narly made a box and told everyone to put a story in it. After a day, she reached into the box and pulled out . . . a snake. She screamed and threw it. The snake flew up in the air, did a somersault and landed on Narly's head. The End. Written by Krusty."

"Ha-ha," I said. "Very funny, Nick."

Nick, Alexander and Buzz howled like hyenas.

"The snake part was great," Alexander said. "I could draw that."

Carly grabbed the paper and stuffed it into her back pocket. "Moving right along." With a red face, she opened seven more blank papers. Then she opened a blank graphic organizer.

"That's by me," Omar said. "I think we should use it to brainstorm ideas."

Carly crumpled it, which I think hurt Omar's feelings. She opened up the last paper. It was printed out from a

computer. "Finally. This looks ~~profesional~~," *professional*
she said.

"Who wrote it?" Tee asked.

Omar didn't want to read it, because he was mad at
Carly for not liking his graphic organizer, so he handed me
the page.

No author's name was on the paper. As I read it, Carly
hopped up and danced around because it was so good.
After two paragraphs, I stopped.

"Why are you stopping?" Carly yelled. "Why isn't
anybody else jumping up and down? This story is
amazing."

Omar said what the rest of us already knew: "That's
from a Mali Koam novel."

"It's from her book called 'Secret Pages,'" Tee added.

Carly looked at Harrison, probably because he is
always reading Mali Koam books during free time. "Did
you do this?"

Poor Harrison looked shocked. "No."

Nick started howling again. "I can't believe I got you."

"Nick!" Carly threw the papers at him. "You ruined it,"
she said, and stormed away.

Not a happy ending.

Dear Kristin,

Your report of what happened was very good. However, "Not a happy ending" is another sentence fragment, not a sentence. It should be "The recess did not end happily."

— Omar

Dear Omar,

Mrs. Penrose said that if you're writing a formal thing like a report, you need complete sentences. If you're writing something creative that has a voice, then you can use sentence fragments. I don't mind if you correct the spelling in here, but don't try to make everybody's writing style like your own. Different strokes for different folks. I like "Not a happy ending." It has a rhythm that fits.

—Kristen

Hi Carly,

   This is Tee. I can tell that you're sad and mad about the whole thing with your contest. Maybe other people didn't have ideas, like me, or just felt too shy. I think Harrison isn't writing yet because he needs time to get comfortable in his new home, like Benjamin in "Secret Pages." I want us all to go back to being good friends.

   It's Halloween! So let's just have fun today. After lunch, we get to put on our Halloween costumes and have a parade and a party. I bet you have a creative costume.

Your friend,
Tee

Dear Carly,

Nick was trying to get a laugh. Let it roll off you. As my mom says, don't cry over spilled grape juice—unless you spill it on a white couch.

I know you were just trying with your contest, but it was kind of awkward for us because it was a competition. I don't mind competing against other strangers in the big contest, but I don't really want to compete against my friends. I liked it better when we were all going to write a story together.

—Kristen

P.S. I'm going to tell Nick he owes you an apology.

Yo Carly,

   Roses are red

   Cherries aren't blue

   Sorry for the blank papers

   And the snake story, too.

      — Nick

Thanks, Nick. I feel better, but not all the way, because we didn't get a story.

      — Carly

You'll Never Guess Who Saves the Day

by Kristin

During morning free time, Mrs. Penrose called me up to her desk.

"What's going on?" she asked. "I thought you'd all be excited for the Halloween party this afternoon, but everyone seems distracted and gloomy. Does this have something to do with the book?"

"Everybody's kind of sad—especially Carly—because we didn't write a big story together," I said. "We kind of gave up."

She thought for a moment. Then she said, "Let's ask Harrison if he has any ideas."

"He doesn't say much," I said.

"Let's try," she said. "Still waters run deep."

We walked over to Harrison's desk. He was finished with our morning work on personification, so he was reading a novel.

"Excuse us," Mrs. Penrose said, and Harrison looked up from his book.

Everybody in the room was staring. Even the pencils were curious.

"It seems that the class would still like to write a collaborative story," Mrs. Penrose said. "Do you have any ideas that might help, Harrison?"

(Hold on. Alexander wants to finish writing this.)

<u>Tick, tick, tick,</u> sang the clock.

Omar's hand crept into the air.

"Hold that thought, Omar," Mrs. Penrose said. "I'd like to hear from Harrison first."

The spotlight was burning on Harrison's face, and I wanted to put him out of his misery. But then he spoke. "I know how Mali Koam gets good ideas for her stories," he said.

The entire room held its breath.

The usually silent Harrison went on. "On her website, Mali Koam says that she never gets good ideas when she is staring at a blank page. She takes her writer's notebook and gets good ideas when she is walking." He looked around at all of us. "Maybe we could take a walk with our book. We could all get ideas and then pick one to work on together."

Silence.

Who knew so many words were ready to pour out of the new guy?

Then Mrs. Penrose said, "Touchdown Twist!"

We all jumped into position and did this crazy twist dance that goes down and up and at the end you put your hands in the air and yell "Touchdown!"

It's what we do when somebody has a particularly great idea.

Harrison looked at us as if we were insane. And then he smiled.

"Can we go on a walk tomorrow?" Jazmine asked.

"Tomorrow is a day off school, and on Monday we have a busy day, but we can go on Tuesday," Mrs. Penrose said.

"Nobody tell anybody else about this walk idea," Carly said. "It'll be our secret strategy to get a story idea and win that contest."

Thanks to Harrison, we have a new, secret plan.

And now ... without further ado ... it is time for recess, lunch and then ... Halloween party time!

Mwa, ha ha. Guess who is now writing in the top-secret book?

Ever since you all said, "This is a private meeting," I have been spying and watching for my opportunity to steal this book. I got it today at recess when Alexander temporarily left the book by the tree.

A story contest. How fascinating.

I happen to be an outstanding writer. I will write a killer story and win.

— Marcos (from Mr. Suarez's class)

Marcos!
— Lauren

I'll write one too! May the best story win!
— Dee Nice

Alexander!

How could you let them steal the book? I'm glad we got it back, but it's too late. Our secret is out. Now everybody from Mr. Suarez's class is gonna enter! What are we gonna do?

—Carly

What can we do? We can write the best story ever. On Tuesday we're going to go for a walk and come up with a great idea. In the meantime, it's Halloween parade and party time!

—Jazmine

Let the ghoulish, ghostly, ghastly rumpus begin!

Halloween

This is Isabella. I am telling the story of the party!

Some moms and dads and my abuelita come after lunch. It is time to put our costumes on.

Omar says, "What's your costume, Mrs. Penrose?"

"I want it to be a surprise," she says. "Isabella, can you help me?"

I feel good that she ~~ask~~ asked me. She gets a bag and we go out to the hallway together. It is special in the hallway with just me and her.

She shows me her costume. She wants to see if I think it is funny and not scary. She knows I don't like scary things. I know everybody will love it. I help her put it on. Then I walk in and say, "Drumroll, please."

Everybody drums and Mrs. Penrose comes in wearing a black cape and fangs. She is a vampire!

"Mwa-ha-ha," she says.

Everybody laughs. Even my abuelita!

"Now I want to do _my_ surprise," Nick says.

We know what Nick is going to be except for Mrs. Penrose, so we say, "Please let him surprise you."

She lets him go to the hallway with one of the moms.

We want to see Mrs. Penrose's face.

Then the door opens. It is Nick. He has on a brown

wig of long hair, glasses, lipstick, a purple dress. He has a pillow stuffed inside for a fake baby.

You're
"~~Your~~ me!" Mrs. Penrose says.

I laugh so hard my cheeks hurt.

Hooray, Isabella! I love your story!
—Tee

This is Jazmine. Here's what we are:

Alexander is . . . . a zombie werewolf.

Carly is . . . . a rich Hollywood movie star.

Tee is . . . . a cat.

Buzz is . . . . . . Pelé, the soccer star from Brazil.

Kristin is . . . . Laura Ingalls Wilder.

Omar is . . . . .the President of the United States. (I have on a whole suit with a Minnesota state flag in my pocket because I never want to forget where I grew up.)

Jazmine is . . . . a cute ladybug.

Harrison is . . . . Benjamin, the character from "Secret Pages."

Isabella is . . . . a doctor.

It's Kristin now. I want to write about the toast. Not bread in the toaster. It's when you clink your glasses.

Ms. Yang came to our room to see us in our costumes.

"Let's have a toast and drink some blood," Mrs. Penrose said, and she pulled red fruit punch out of the closet.

"Happy Halloween," Mrs. Penrose said. "Everybody say 'Cheers!'" We all said it and clinked our cups.

Then we did a toast in Spanish for Isabella (¡Salud!), in Vietnamese for Tee (Yô), in Arabic for Omar (Be ṣaḥtak), in Hmong for Ms. Yang (Txhais key zoo siab) and in Swedish for me, Kristin (Skål).

Tee said, "Let's make a special toast to the baby." She held up her cup, and then she panicked. "I can't think of what to say."

"Happy baby!" Jazmine said.

"Happy baby!" we all said, and clinked.

"Can I clink the baby?" Nick asked.

Mrs. Penrose laughed and said, "Sure."

Isabella got worried, because she thought Nick would do it too hard. But Nick clinked his cup on Mrs. Penrose's stomach softly and everybody laughed.

Then we all clinked on Nick's fake baby pillow.

Look at this! Too many messes are happening in this book! Did anybody see who did this? I bet it was Nick.

Dude. Wasn't me.—*Nick*

Perhaps it was made by a ghost!
— *Alexander H. Gory, Jr.*

I did it. I am very very very sorry.— Isabella

It's okay, Isabella. Everybody makes mistakes.
— *Tee*

Hey,

              everybody
  Welcome back, ~~everbody~~. Happy November!
Tomorrow we go on our walk to get a story
idea. Get your brains ready. We're going to
write a better story than Marcos or DeeNice or
anybody, and win this contest.

                 — Carly

                          stolen
P.S. No leaving this book where it can get ~~stealed~~.

  Snow is coming tonight. Maybe it will be dangerous.
If Mrs. Penrose falls down that will be bad for the baby.
                 — Isabella

Even if it does snow, exercise is good for bodies and babies. My mom exercised all the time right before I was born, and she said I came out as strong and healthy as a horse.

—Kristen

If it snows, I hope we can still go, because I really want to get a good idea for a story.

—Tee

I want to go on a brainstorming walk, too, but I also want it to snow, because I've never seen snow. It never snowed in Miami, where I'm from.

—Harrison

I hope it snows for Harrison, since he wants it to and since he's the one who told us about Mali Koam.

—Alexander

Thanks.—Harrison

It snowed the right amount!!!! Hurray!!!

To the Whole Class,

1. It snowed 2.5 inches.

2. We are on a walk right now. Our minds are bubbling with ideas.

3. I am creating a graphic organizer. I'm going to pass it from person to person. Write down one story idea this walk is giving you. I will do the first one as an example. Then we can vote on which one to use for our big story.

Sincerely,
Omar

P.S. No smudges, please.

Results of Our Hike Around the School Building

Name One Story Idea You Are Getting

Omar—A class at Delite Elementary School in Minnesota takes a hike by the creek on a snowy day.

Jazmine—Snow fairies!

Tee—I'm not sure what to write. That rabbit we saw in the snow on the bank of the creek is staying in my mind. I'd like to write about that, but I don't know what could happen to make it a good story.

Alexander—A mysterious boy named Elaxendar makes a Zombie Owl out of snow that can fly.

Nick—Frosty, the Zombie Snow Owl, flies in our window, and he melts and all that's left are his black eyes, and a girl named Krusty thinks they're chocolate chips and eats them. Ha-ha.

Kristin—I've heard that the eyeballs of Zombie Owls are delicious and nutritious, Nick. I will make sure Santa puts some in your stocking. But that's not what I wanted to write for my idea. Here is my idea: A pioneer girl gets lost in a snowstorm. (Snow from a branch just landed on the page, and it made a smudge when I wiped it off. Sorry, Omar. You can't control Mother Nature.)

Buzz—School is closed forever and we have a snowball fight.

Harrison—It never stops snowing, and huge mountains of snow form, and we can walk on top of them in silence except for the crunching of our feet in the snow, and we are so high up we can touch the moon with our fingertips.

This is Alexander again. I just wanted to say that even though Harrison's idea doesn't have any ghosts or vampires, it gave me a chill up my spine because of the way he wrote it.

Isabella—I got nothing. Except maybe frostbite.

Carly—I think a lot of these would win. Let's vote on one tomorrow.

Nick's Story

Krusty was going to write, but I'm in the mood, dudes. So let me tell y'all what's going down.

Indoor recess today because of freezing rain. Oh joy.

Mrs. Penrose is sitting at her desk reading a book about babies. We're sitting on the floor in the Good Book Nook having a jolly argument.

Krusty made us take a secret vote by writing down the story we wanted to work on. Problem? Everybody voted for their own idea, which meant nobody won.

Awkward!

What did we do next? Argue argue, blah blah, yada yada, shmada shmada.

Finally Harrison came up with an idea. "Why don't we just write to Mali Koam and ask for advice?"

"A famous author won't write us back," Isabella said.

"Come on, it's worth a try," Carly said.

Then Omar, that daring, adventurous fellow, said, "We have to ask Mrs. Penrose first."

Immediately Mrs. Penrose said yes. She loved the idea.

By the way, I have written a nonfiction book about babies. It's educational. I will put a copy of it here for free.

Babies

by Nick the Slick

Babies. They drool. They burp. They sleep. They cry. They poop. The End.

If I were sitting in a chair, I would be falling off it, I am laughing so hard. I would buy that book.

— Buzz

Nick,

Hilarious! Mrs. Penrose was just teaching us about sarcasm this morning, and you used it. Very clever. I'm not being sarcastic. I mean it.

— Alexander H. Gory, Jr.

Dear Friends,

Writing a letter to an author! What an exciting project! Why don't you write your drafts in here? I'll help you mail the final letters, and we'll include a stamped envelope with our school's address on it to make it easier for her to write back to us. Ms. Yang is going to be over the moon about this idea.

Your teacher,
Mrs. Penrose

I guess it's okay for Mrs. Penrose to tell Ms. Yang, but nobody tell anybody else about this. Especially ~~Espeshatly~~ DeeNice and Marcos.

— Carly

Hey,

                               author

    Here is my secret letter to the ~~auther~~.

We'll get secret advice so we can use it to make

the best story and win.

                          — Carly

Dear Mali ~~Koom~~ Koam,

My name is Carly Grace Winston, and

I have three sisters and a cat named Big Foot.

I used to have a gerbil, but it ~~exscaped~~ escaped and it

~~protty~~ probably got ~~ate~~ eaten by the cat. Are you a ~~famus~~ famous writer

or just a regular one? Almost everyone in our class

reads all your books. Tee told me to check out

"Fur" from the ~~libary~~ library, but I didn't read it

because the cover looked boooooring.

We want to write a big story and win a

contest. Please tell us how to do it. We want to

get rich and ~~famus~~ famous.

Yours truly,

Carly

P.S. Please put your ~~autograf~~ autograph on this line so I

can sell it and make some money.

_____

To Carly:

1. Your letter was bad.
2. You didn't even spell the author's name right.
3. I vote that Mrs. Penrose should NOT mail your letter.
4. We should all write one letter.
5. I will make a graphic organizer.

Sincerely,
Omar

Hey, Omar,

Mind your own beeswax.

Yours truly,
Carly

Hi!

This is supposed to be fun! ☺ We can all write letters if we want. Mrs. Penrose says that we can help each other make our writing better, in a nice way. Remember CBC (Compliment Before Criticizing)? We are supposed to say something nice first and then give our concrete suggestion for making it better.

Hugs,

Jazmine

To Carly,

1. Your letter to Mali Koam was lively.
2. Fix your spelling.
3. Take out the part about the cover being boring.

Sincerely,

Omar

Dear Carly,

You have a lot of fun energy. Mali Koam's feelings might be hurt about the cover part.

Best wishes,
Tee

P.S. I want to write a letter, but I can't think of what to say.

Greetings, Carly,

I didn't like the cover of "Fur" at all. It was too sunshiny. I loved the book, though. I am writing my own letter to Mali Koam.

— Alexander H. Gory, Jr.

P.S. The name of your cat is fantastic. Big Foot! That is called irony, because cats have little feet. Mrs. Penrose was just teaching us about irony yesterday. Here is my letter.

Dear Mali Koam,

You are a good writer, but you should write more scary stories. Also you should put more dramatic and frightening drawings on your covers to attract attention.

I am putting in my drawing for a new cover for your book "Fur." What do you think?

Someone else in my class asked you how to make a story great, so I won't ask you that. Instead I will give you some good news that should make you excited. When I die, I will haunt your house, because then you will have a fantastic scary story to write. You are welcome.

Your humble servant,
Alexander H. Gory, Jr.

Hey,

I corrected the spelling parts in my letter to Mali Koam. But I left in the part about the boring cover, because it's the truth and nothing but the truth. I can't wait until she writes back.

— Carly

Don't get up all your hopes. She is probably busy writing more books.

— Isabella

Isabella might be right on this one. I'm going to wait and see if she writes back before I spend time on a letter. That is the practical thing to do.

— Kristen

Yo Peeps,

I believe an author would appreciate an original poem.

Here is my letter to Mali Koam.

Dear Mali Koam,

Violets are blue.

Roses are red.

How many books

Do you have in your head?

Yours drooly,
Nick the Funnyman

P.S. Did your fingers fall off from writing so much? Now do you write with your toes?

LOL!
— Carly

Dear Author,

Roses are red.

Violets are tall.

Please keep your books

And send me a ball.

From,
Buzz Benson

LOL again!
— Carly

To the Whole Class:

Buzz's poem was not appropriate at all. Mrs. Penrose brainstormed with us what should go into a letter this morning. Here is what a letter to an author should include:

1. The date.

2. The greeting (such as "Dear Author").

3. A sentence about yourself.

4. A sentence telling the author one thing you liked about one of his or her books.

5. A serious question.

6. The closing (such as "Sincerely").

Sincerely,
Omar

Okay. Here is my serious question for the author:

Who wants to sit around and write all day.

— Buzz

To Buzz:

1. Bad question.

2. It doesn't even have a question mark.

Sincerely,
Omar

Yo Goys and Birls,

Buzz has a good question. Who wants to sit around and write all day?

Answer: People with extra padding in their bottoms. Ha-ha. Just kidding.

Ta-ta for now now,
Nick

Hi,

    I think it was good that Buzz wrote something in this book. He wasn't serious about sending that poem to Mali Koam. Nobody would want to hurt her feelings. I also think Omar's list of things to put in an author letter is helpful. I would add the thing that Mrs. Penrose has up on the wall: "Voice: Let your personality come through in your writing."
    I worked on my letter to Mali Koam. Here it is.

Yours truly,

Tee

Dear Mali Koam,

   My name is Tee. I love to read, and I am burning to write. My favorite book is "Fur." I loved your description of the river and how the bear felt in the morning. It was like you were writing about me. But I am not a bear. But I am like the bear on the inside. I want to make someone feel as if I am writing down their soul on the paper.

   My problem is when I look at blank paper, I get a terrible ache in my stomach. I don't know how to get an idea for a whole story. We took a walk like you do, and I saw a rabbit and thought a story about that would be good, but then my mind goes empty. I think I was born without an imagination.

Best wishes for a fascinating life,

Tee

(My real name is Thi Linh Nguyen, but I'm called Tee.)

P.S. Do you have any pets? I was a cat for Halloween. I don't have any pets or any little sisters or brothers even though I want one, but my teacher is going to have a baby.

Great letter, Tee. Here is my letter!

Hi, Mali Koam,

Thank you for writing such great books!
Hurray! Hurray!! Please make more
books!!!!

—Jazmine

Dear Mali Koam,

My name is Harrison. I am a new student at Delite Elementary School in Delite, Minnesota. I moved here from Miami because my mom got a job at Rasmussen College, and I miss the palm trees and the ocean and my best friend, whose name is Aaron and who loves to read as much as me. I miss my old school, too. There aren't as many kids here that look like me and that made me feel different. At first I didn't like anything about Minnesota. Now I like two things. First, I like the snow. When it snows, my backyard looks like a big, blank white page. Whenever the snow is fresh, I put on my boots and write a big message in the snow by making tracks of the letters with my feet. It doesn't matter if anybody ever sees it. I know it's there. (Yesterday I wrote the word "Salutations," like Charlotte.) The other thing I like is this book we have in our class. I haven't written much in it, but I like to read it when nobody is looking.

My favorite book of yours is "Secret Pages." I've read it seventeen times. When I get to the part about Benjamin finding the book inside the tree trunk from that secret friend, I want to turn the page to read what happens, but I also don't want to turn the page because I don't want the story to end. I feel this incredible buzzing in my chest. It is the same feeling I get when I am about to open up a birthday present. I want to tear off the wrapping paper, but I also don't want my birthday to be over.

My question is: Did all the things that happen in your books happen to you in real life? Did a secret friend leave a book for you inside a tree?

Your fan,
Harrison

Dear Harrison,

Your letter to Mali Koam was fantastic. It made me want to read "Secret Pages," which I haven't read yet.

Respectfully yours,
Alexander H. Gory, Jr.

P.S. You can come sledding with me and my brothers the next time we have a big snow. Minnesota has some really fun things. In the summer you can go to the state fair or you can go to Spirit Mountain in Duluth. Or you can go up north. We go to Lake Winnibigoshish. We stay in a creepy cabin that once had a bat in it.

Dear Alexander H. Gory, Jr.,

Thank you for the compliment and the travel tips. I have a copy of "Secret Pages" if you would like to borrow it. There are no scary parts, but there are suspenseful parts.

From,
Harrison

Harrison,

I know how you feel about moving. I came here in Kindergarten. You feel alone at first and then it gets better.

—Isabella

To the Whole Class:

1. I wrote a rough draft of my letter to Mali Koam and gave it to Mrs. Penrose for feedback.

2. Mali Koam lives in Maryland, which is approximately 1,285 miles away. MN is for Minnesota. MD is for Maryland. Did you know there are eight states that begin with "M"? I know all of them and their postal abbreviations.

3. I also have a miniature state flag collection. I have all of the states, including Maryland.

4. Tonight I will revise my letter and put a copy in here tomorrow.

Sincerely,
Omar

Omar Abdi Samatar
c/o Mrs. Penrose
Delite Elementary School
404 Larsen Avenue
Delite, MN 55125
November 14

Dear Mali Koam,

My name is Omar Abdi Samatar. On my last report card, I got all A's. My hobbies are playing the piano, collecting state flags and coins and reading nonfiction and fiction. I have read ten of your books and plan to read the other two soon. I give you an A+ on your word choice so far. Keep up the great work.

My serious question is: If we write a story to enter in a contest, should we do the three-step process?

- Brainstorm (I like graphic organizers)

- Write a rough draft

- Revise

Some people in my class just want to write and say they're done.

Sincerely,
Omar

Greetings, Fellow Classmates,

Mailing a letter is like automatically making suspense. During our morning lesson on oxymorons, I imagined my letter slowly zipping from Minnesota to Maryland. Will it reach Mali Koam? Will she read it? Will she write an unbelievably real letter back to me with her very own hands?

Almost exactly twenty-four hours ago, Mrs. Penrose helped Harrison, Nick, Carly, Jazmine, Tee and me mail fresh copies of our letters. I know it's seriously ridiculous to expect a letter back already, but I can't wait.

Jiggily yours,
Alexander H. Gory, Jr.

Dear Boys and Girls,

I asked Alexander for permission to write in here. I just wanted to share some fun news. Lately, when you are out at recess and I am sitting quietly at my desk, I often feel the baby kicking. It feels as if I have swallowed a little dinosaur. A nice dinosaur, to be sure. It's thrilling.

Your teacher,
Mrs. Penrose

Kicking? I told you he's going to be a striker.

— Buzz

Maybe <u>she's</u> going to be a striker! The baby might be a girl. Mrs. Penrose, please please, tell us if you know. Is it a boy or a girl?

—Jazmine

As long as the baby is healthy, it doesn't matter if it's a boy or a girl. But . . . I did find out, and it's a boy.

— Mrs. Penrose

Our teacher is always for us

She would never bore us

Now she is having

a baby stegosaurus!
—Guess who?

LOL—Carly

Your baby boy can't wait to meet us!
—Tee

We can't wait for two things: for Mrs. Penrose's baby and for Mali Koam's letters!
—Jazmine

Hey,

Big trouble! I saw DeeNice in the bathroom and she said, "How's your story?" I said, "Great." So she showed me her notebook. Her story was five pages long and she said she is still writing! Five pages already! I think we should just pick an idea and write a story for that contest. Let's just go, go, go.

—Carly

To the Whole Class:

1. Just because DeeNice has written five pages doesn't mean the writing is good.

2. We are going to get professional advice from a real writer.

3. The deadline for that contest is at the end of December. We have time!

4. As soon as we get advice from Mali Koam, we'll write a rough draft and then we can revise it and send it in.

Sincerely,
Omar

No letters from Mali Koam. Mrs. Penrose said that we shouldn't expect anything until December! Waiting is difficult.

—Tee

Mwa ha ha. Guess who?

I have written eleven pages. On the computer!

—*Marcos*

I am burning mad. Marcos got the book this morning on the bus! I'm sorry, but he was as sneaky as a snake.

— *Alexander*

Oh no! Now he knows about Mali Koam!
—*Tee*

No. He wrote in it, but he didn't have time to read much because I grabbed it back.

— *Alexander*

11 pages on the computer! My heart is busted in pieces.

—*Carly*

Sad Greetings,

Marcos said on the bus that he finished his story over the weekend and entered it in the contest. We are doomed.

— Alexander H. Gory, Jr.

Come on, guys! We can't give up!

Today is our last day before Thanksgiving break. Everybody should get in a good mood. Eat turkey! Eat pie with whipped cream! Be thankful!

When we come back, I bet we'll get helpful letters from Mali Koam. Then we'll write our story and send it in. Then, Mrs. Penrose will have a cute itty-bitty baby boy and bring him in and it will be a really, really happy and fun spring!

Happy Turkey Day, everybody!

Hugs, Jazmine

Question: What did the turkey say to the chicken on Thanksgiving?

Answer: You're clucky you're not a turkey.

— Nick the Slick

Ha! Okay, I'm cheered up. If I were a turkey, guess what I'd do at Thanksgiving? Wear a chicken disguise.

— Alexander H. Gory, Jr.

Alexander is a turkey.

I did not draw this. My little brother did this! I can draw way better.

I think it's a good drawing for a kindergartner.
— Tee

I think we should keep the book away from little kids because they will mess it up.
— Omar

A bleak and depressing return from break. No letters from Mali Koam.

— Alexander H. Gory, Jr.

It wasn't bleak or depressing!
We got to feel the baby kick!

— Jazmine

Crazy Time

by Kristin

We have been on pins and needles, as my mom says. That doesn't mean we've been sitting on them for real. It's what Mrs. Penrose calls an idiom. We're anxious and excited about a lot of things: getting advice from Mali Koam, the competition from DeeNice and Marcos, Christmas coming, the baby, and more! And even more things have been happening. Here's a quick update. Wait. Nick just said he wants to do it.

Update on Last Week

On Monday during math class Omar got the flu.

On Tuesday the germs attacked Alexander, too.

Then Buzz sprained his ankle playing soccer on the ice.

On Wednesday the fire alarm went off twice.

On Thursday night we had our concert singing fa-la-la-ly!

A baby burped in the middle, which I thought was fa-la-jolly.

On Friday Mr. Suarez's pet snake got loose.

All the classes looked for him, but it was no use.

Then Isabella screamed and her eyes went buggy.

"Look!" she yelled. The snake was hiding in her cubby.

— *Nick the Poet*

(yeah, baby, I know it)

Great News!

Ms. Yang came with mail from the office. Mali Koam wrote back to me, Alexander, Nick and Harrison. Really! Mrs. Penrose made copies of the letters so everybody can read them. I'm keeping my real letter to sell on eBay. I don't think she's that famous, but maybe I could get five bucks for it.

Not richly yours yet,
Carly

P.S. Omar, I spelled famous right. I used to spell it famus.

Dear Carly,

Thank you for your letter. I'm sorry that you disliked the cover of my book. To tell you the truth, I didn't like the cover either. Often, writers do not get to choose their book covers. The publishers do that because they're the ones paying for the book to be produced. My hope is that you'll take a chance and crack it open. Once you get past the cover, you might enjoy it. As they say, you can't judge a book by its cover.

As for getting rich quick by writing books, I'm afraid I don't have good news. It took me ten years of writing before I got my first book published. Even though I have published twelve books, I am not rich. Writing is hard work. I wake up every day and write from nine to five o'clock (with a break for a walk and lunch). Although I don't make a lot of money, I love my work.

Happy reading,
Mali Koam

Dear Alexander,

Thank you for your thoughtful offer to haunt me. That's a first. You clearly enjoy a thrilling read, and you are inspiring me to consider writing a scary story. The problem is I am a big chicken.

The illustration you included was terrific and terrifying. Excellent work.

I hope you keep reading, writing and drawing.

Take care,
Mali Koam

Dear Nick,

Thank you for the hilarious poem. I laughed out loud when I read your question about my fingers falling off from writing so much. What an idea for a funny and ghoulish story that you should write!

You obviously have a great sense of humor. I hope you use it to write many wonderful stories.

Yours,
Mali Koam

Dear Harrison,

Your words made my day. I loved your description of how it feels when you get to an exciting part of a book. Beautiful writing. I can tell that we are kindred spirits. When I was your age, I moved to a new school. I was shy and didn't make friends easily. I discovered that whenever I was lonely, I could open a book and disappear into another world. I wanted to capture that feeling in "Secret Pages."

I didn't really have a secret friend who left me a book inside a tree trunk. Sometimes authors write the stories they wish had happened. I wanted Benjamin to not only find a friend in a book, but also to find a friend in his life.

May you always have good books to read. And may you find a kindred spirit in your new school.

Your fellow writer,
Mali Koam

Surprised and Shocked

by Kristin

Carly, Nick, Alexander and Harrison were all jumping around. It was fun to read the letters from Mali Koam out loud. The boys let us hold theirs, but Carly wouldn't.

"It'll be worth less with fingerprints on it," she said.

"Wow," Isabella said. "I really can't believe it."

"I'm glad I didn't bet on it," I said.

Then we noticed how sad Tee looked.

"Don't worry, Tee," Mrs. Penrose said. "Your reply will come. We mailed the letters from you, Omar and Jazmine later than theirs."

"But Christmas is coming," Tee said. "What if we don't get our letters before the break?"

"We still have next week," Jazmine said. "Our letters will come."

Omar is dying to write, so I'm going to turn this over to him.

To the Whole Class:

We are getting a lot of good information from Mali Koam. We need to keep track of it. Please write below one thing you learned from her. I did an example.

Sincerely,
Omar

Things We Learned from Mali Koam's Letters

1. You can't judge a book by it's cover.— Omar

2. Hey Omar, you made a mistake. Ha-ha. It should be: You can't judge a book by its cover. Oh, and here's what I learned from Mali Koam: The best part of an author's day is lunch.— Nick

3. Writing is hard work. Authors write every day from 9 to 5 o'clock and don't make much money.— Kristen

4. I need to go into real estate.— Carly

5. An author is nice for taking time out of her busy day to write letters. —Jazmine

6. My illustrations are terrifying and terrific.
(Also, Friday the 13th can be a lucky day.)
— Alexander H. Gory, Jr.

7. Authors are real people. (I hope she writes back
to me, too.)— Tee

8. Mali Koam is excellent at writing
letters in addition to books. I knew she
would be.—Harrison

9. **Being a writer is a sad and lonely life.**
— Buzz

10. At first, I am thinking Mrs. Penrose wrote the
letters and pretends they were from Mali Koam so we
won't be sad but then Omar shows me the postmark from
Maryland. What I learn is sometimes when you write a
letter to someone, you get a letter back.— Isabella

Dear Omar,

I noticed you got very quiet after Nick found your
mistake. Don't feel bad about it. Everybody makes
mistakes. It makes me sad when someone in our
room is sad, so I hope this makes you feel better.

Your friend,
Tee

Dear Tee,

1. I am very embarrassed.

2. Everybody is probably laughing at me inside.

3. I don't think I should write in here anymore.

Sincerely,
Omar

Dear Omar,

When Nick wrote "ha-ha," he wasn't really laughing. You know Nick. I think he was pointing out what Mrs. Penrose called irony. It was ironic that you made a mistake because you're usually so perfect. Look at it this way. You did us all a big favor by making a mistake. You showed us that everybody is human.

—Kristen

Omar,

Keep writing in here. If we're going to win this contest, we need ya.

— Carly

Okay, y'all.— Omar

Ha-ha. Good one, dude.— Nick

Hurray!!! It's like Christmas!!!!! Omar
and I got letters!!!! Hurray!!!!

— From the Desk of Mali Koam —

Dear Jazmine,

   Thank you for your note and your encouragement.
Your snazzy, jazzy pictures on the envelope really made
my day.

                         Keep reading and writing,
                         Mali Koam

Dear Omar,

I'm delighted that you have read so many of my books. Now, on to your fascinating question about the writing process. Is revision necessary?

Whether or not I revise depends on what I'm writing. If I'm writing just for fun or writing in my diary, I don't need to revise. But if I want to share my writing with the world, I want it to be the best it can be. The truth is that my first try at a story is usually bad. I am just getting my ideas down. So, I have to revise all of my stories.

I believe that writers are a lot like athletes. Let's say you are a soccer player and you want to do a bicycle kick. You know that you won't get it right on the first try. You have to do that bicycle kick over and over in order to get good at it. A coach might give you some helpful comments on how to improve. An athlete needs to have a good attitude, listen to those comments and work hard. When you watch a great athlete, you can see how much focus and energy he or she is putting into it.

When it's time for me to revise, I imagine I'm an Olympic athlete and the whole world is watching to see if I can nail this revision. I don't say, "Oh, forget it. My rough draft was good enough. Revising is a waste of time." Instead, I say to myself, "Come on, Mali Koam! You can do this better. Come on, baby! Go big or go home!" Then I write with everything I've got.

I hope that helps.

Write on,
Mali Koam

I couldn't believe that author lady knows what a bicycle kick is. And she said go big or go home. That's what I say! I might read one of her books someday.— Buzz

"Come on, baby!" cracked me up.— Nick

Will she ever write back to me?— Tee

WOW

by Kristin

Right in the middle of our lesson on allusions, Ms. Yang burst in.

"Pardon the interruption, but the mail came." She waved an envelope, and she had a smile on her face. "Ho ho ho!"

"Oooh," Mrs. Penrose said, and looked at Tee. "I have a feeling someone is going to be happy."

Ms. Yang gave Tee the envelope.

"It's from Mali Koam!" Tee said, and started jumping up and down. Tee is tiny, so she is extra cute when she does that.

"Would you like to read it to us?" Mrs. Penrose asked.

Tee nodded. First she just held the letter in her hands, and then she read it to us.

Dear Tee,

When I was your age, I used to be afraid of blank paper, too. I wanted to write stories, but I didn't have any ideas. The longer I stared at the paper, the more afraid I would become. One day, my teacher said we could write a play. I went home sick because I couldn't face it.

I overcame my fear, and you can, too. I will teach you my trick. It is simple. I call it the WOW trick. It is not the only way to write a story, but it is a way to write a great, simple story.

You start with a character that wants something. That is the first W. Then, there is an obstacle that gets in the way. That is the O. Finally, the character finds a way to overcome the obstacle and get whatever he or she wants. I call that the win. That is the final W. WOW.

You don't have to think of a story all at once. You just have to start with the question: Who is my character and what does my character want?

Imagine my character is a nice cat. What might a nice cat want? A saucer of milk? What might get in the way of a cat wanting milk? A mean dog? How could the nice cat get around the mean dog and win the milk in the end? Trick the mean dog into leaving? Get help from a friend? Sing the mean dog a lullaby until he falls asleep? I bet you could think of a WOW outline for your rabbit. Give it a try.

Your fellow writer,
Mali Koam

P.S. If you get stuck, don't stare at the blank paper. Close your eyes and really picture where your main character is and then open your eyes and write your first sentence.

Greetings,

See? There has to be an obstacle—that's the scary part, the suspenseful part. Without the O, there isn't a story. I've been trying to explain that for years.

Overjoyed about obstacles,
Alexander H. Gory, Jr.

I'm so excited because the WOW trick is giving me ideas. I'm thinking about that rabbit we saw on our walk. I could have the rabbit <u>want</u> to visit a friend, but the <u>obstacle</u> could be a storm that gets in the way, and then he could somehow find his friend in the end for the <u>win</u>.

—Tee

Make it a <u>she</u> rabbit.— Jazmine

I want to make it a <u>he</u> because Mrs. Penrose's baby is a <u>he</u>.—Tee

What if the storm made a flood and the rabbit had to fight for his life in the water? That would make us want to turn the page. I agree with Alexander. The more suspense there is, the bigger the <u>win</u> will be.

—Harrison

Make the storm ferocious!— Alexander

I can't wait to write it. Thanks, everybody. When I close my eyes, I can see the whole thing like it's real.

—Tee

Breaking News

by Alexander H. Gory, Jr.

Marcos from Mr. Suarez's class stopped me just now on the way to the bathroom.

"Did you guys enter your story in that contest yet?" he asked with a Slytherin scowl.

"Maybe. Maybe not," I said.

"Tell Carly that Mrs. Nowlopp, Mrs. Czekyour and Ms. Sonnel found out about the contest and they're giving extra credit to everybody in their classes for entering."

Even more competition for us.

We are certainly doomed now.

Emergency

by Kristin

When Alexander brought us the news, we asked
Mrs. Penrose for a class meeting.

"This is bad, bad, bad," Carly said.

"Competition is a part of life," Mrs. Penrose said.
"You have two choices. You can either give up or you
can stay in the game and do your best."

"Who cares about them?" Jazmine said. "Let's just
have fun."

Carly got excited again. "Okay, but I still think we
have a better chance of winning if we work together. Ten
heads are better than one."

"We can always write our own stories for fun, but
if we all work on one for the contest together, then we
won't be competing against each other," Tee said.

"We'll never agree on a story idea," Omar said.
"We have completely different tastes, in case you didn't
notice."

"Let's each write down one WOW idea and put it in
a hat," I suggested. "We'll pick one. Whatever we pick,
we'll do. No moaning and groaning if we don't pick yours.
We can make any subject into a good story. And like Tee
said, you can always write your own story at home."

"Very practical suggestion, Kristin," Mrs. Penrose said.

"Whoever's story gets picked can start writing the story. Then he or she can pass it on. We can all add to it," Harrison suggested.

"Like a relay race," Buzz said.

Isabella jumped up and got her hat out of her cubby. She has a very cute purple one with flowers on it. "We can put our ideas in here."

"Wait. Can I please suggest how to write the ideas?" Omar asked.

"Sure," Mrs. Penrose said.

"Everybody write your idea in three sentences." Omar went up to the smartboard and wrote:

1. Who is your character and what does your character want?

2. What is the obstacle that gets in the way of the want?

3. How does the character win?

"Fine," Carly said, and Omar smiled.

We all wrote down our three sentences, folded up our papers, and put them in Isabella's hat.

"Mrs. Penrose," I said. "You pick so that it's fair."

Isabella held out the hat. Mrs. Penrose closed her eyes and picked.

I looked around the room. You could tell that

everybody wanted ~~their~~ ^{his or her} story to be the one, but I think
nobody wanted it as badly as Tee. She had her eyes
closed, too, and you just knew she was picturing that
rabbit in her mind.

Mrs. Penrose pulled a piece of paper out and
opened it.

"The rabbit story!" she said.

Tee jumped up and started doing her little sugarplum
fairy dance again, which made everybody laugh. Even
Nick, who really wanted a funny story, was happy for her.

"I have an idea," Alexander said.

"Let me guess," Carly said. "You want to turn it into a
rabbit zombie."

"Actually, I was thinking about how Harrison got that
idea for a story about the moon and the snow on our
walk," Alexander said. "What if the moon was out, like
Harrison said, and the rabbit thought the moon was his
friend and he wanted to climb up to it. But then he gets
lost and the storm comes—"

Harrison smiled.

"Yeah, but somehow there has to be a happy ending!"
Jazmine said.

"I absolutely love this enthusiasm," Mrs. Penrose said.
Her eyes crinkled the way they do when she likes what
we say. "Tomorrow I'll make sure to set aside time so you
can write a rough draft. I can't wait to read that story."

WOW story coming tomorrow. Stay tuned.
That's a wrap!

Disaster

by Alexander H. Gory, Jr.

Close your eyes. Imagine a whole team of
Olympic speed skaters on the ice, hearts pounding,
muscles gripping, ready to start the race of their lives.

That was us this morning, waiting to come into
the school to work on our WOW story. We were all
talking excitedly as we walked into the room . . . and
then we froze.

A tall, white-haired stranger with a white
mustache and round glasses was sitting at Mrs.
Penrose's desk.

"My name is Mr. Pinkerton," he said. "Put away
your things and sit quietly. We have lots of work to
do today."

"Where is Mrs. Penrose?" Jazmine asked.

His lips were zipped. He wrote on the board: "Mr.
Pinkerton's Rules: 1) If you have a question, please raise
your hand." Then he turned around and looked at us.

Carly dared to raise her hand.

"Will Mrs. Penrose be back tomorrow?"

"I was just given this assignment for today. I assume your teacher will be back tomorrow," Mr. Pinkerton said. Then he started passing out worksheets. "I've taught for many years and have seen every trick in the book. Treat me with respect and we'll get along just fine."

He gave us so much morning work (the lesson was about when to use parentheses), we didn't have any time to write the story. That is not getting along "just fine" to me.

At recess, Tee (dying to start the story) tried to get this book from the shelf in the Good Book Nook, but he took it with the bony fingers of his outstretched hand and put it back on the shelf.

"Mrs. Penrose lets us take it outside," Carly said. "We get to write in it whenever we have free time."

Mr. Pinkerton did not blink. "My rule is no bringing anything out to recess."

We were furious. Tee was almost crying.

"It's okay, Tee," Jazmine said. "Tomorrow we can tell Mrs. Penrose that Mr. Pinkerton wouldn't let us write."

"Yeah," Nick said. "We'll tell her that Mr. Finkerton made us work so hard our fingers fell off."

"What if she can't come back tomorrow?" Isabella asked.

"She probably just went to the doctor for a checkup today," Kristin said.

"I bet she's getting one of those X-ray pictures of the baby," Carly said. "My mom showed me mine. I'm all curled up but I'm looking at the camera and my thumb is like this . . ." Carly smiled and gave us a big thumbs-up sign.

We had to laugh at that one (well, except for Omar).

"That's a lie," Omar said. "Babies have their eyes closed in there."

"Okay, but I had my thumb up, and that is no lie," she said.

I am writing this after school and will have to stop when my bus is called. If Mrs. Penrose doesn't return tomorrow, we must begin ways of plotting to overcome the ornery obstacle known as Mr. Pinkerton!

(Nick is begging for a turn.)

Today the room (Mrs. Penrose's classroom) became a pit of quicksand (not really, of course, that was just a metaphor) and we spent the day sinking. Why, you ask? (Actually, you didn't really ask, but I'm imagining that you're curious.) Because the lesson (taught by Mr. Pinkerton (our substitute)) about parentheses (those handy little hooks that go around a phrase (or a word or a whole sentence))) was so boring.

Ha ha ha ha.

— *Nick* (the King of Parenthesising)

Nick, I get the joke, but it made my eyes hurt.— *Omar*

The Note

by Kristin

I am at home writing in this book! At night! I wanted to write down what happened today, but Mr. Pinkerton gave us so much work there was no free time at the end of the day. I asked Alexander if I should take this book home and he said yes. I'll put it back in the classroom first thing in the morning.

Two big things happened today, both terrible. First, Mrs. Penrose was absent again. The second big thing happened at recess.

We went down to our spot to talk just like we did yesterday.

"Mrs. Penrose is definitely coming back tomorrow," Jazmine said.

"You don't know," Isabella said. "Something with the baby might be bad."

Her sentence made us all stop breathing for a second. Then Carly gave her a mean look and said, "I'm not in the mood for Debbie Downer."

I was mad at Isabella for saying that about the baby,

so I said, "Yeah, do us all a favor and look on the bright side for a change, Isabella."

"Yeah. The baby is fine, so just keep it to yourself, Isabella," Jazmine added.

"How do you know the baby is fine?" Isabella asked.

"Because we aren't gloomy like you," Carly said.

"But everything isn't always happy all the time," Isabella exclaimed. "Bad things happen. You can't always fix them."

The day was freezing, and we were all standing in a huddle between the merry-go-round and the pine tree. Isabella had her hood tight, so you couldn't see any of her black curly hair.

Carly snapped, "What's wrong with you?"

It was like a slap. Isabella's round brown face got reddish on her cheeks. Her eyes got full of tears and she blinked. She was going to say something, and her breath made a puff of steam in the air. Then she turned and started walking silently up the hill toward the blacktop.

"I'm glad," Carly said. "Nobody wants to be around a Debbie Downer."

We just stood there and listened to Isabella's footsteps crunch on the crust of the snow as she walked away.

And then Alexander whispered, "Remember?"

"Remember what?" I asked.

"At the end of second grade, Isabella's mom had a

baby who died. She was Isabella's baby sister."

Nobody said anything. Not even Carly.

Tee went up to be with Isabella. I wanted to go, but my feet froze to the ground.

When we came inside from recess, Jazmine gave Isabella her new purple glitter pen, which is Isabella's favorite color. That gave Carly an idea. She got a purple friendship wristband from her cubby and put it on Isabella's desk. Now I was more frozen, because I am usually the one to come up with great solutions fast.

I was also jealous, because I still want one of those wristbands, and I happen to know Carly has a box full of them in her cubby.

During science, I didn't raise my hand once even though I knew all the answers. I kept staring down at the magnifying glass and the different objects we were supposed to be looking at so that I wouldn't have to see Isabella and so that nobody else would see my face. Mr. Pinkerton didn't even notice. My stomach started to hurt.

After science, Mr. Pinkerton asked Tee to collect all the magnifying glasses, and when she came to my desk, she whispered, "Maybe you could write a note."

I looked up. She knew.

I grabbed a piece of paper. While Mr. Pinkerton was getting everything set up for social studies, I wrote.

Dear Isabella,

    I'm sorry I was mean to you. If I had a baby sister who died, I would be sad. Bad things can happen and that is the truth and the truth is scary.

               Your friend (hopefully),
               Kristen

    I gave it to her when Mr. Pinkerton wasn't looking. Then my heart stopped beating and I couldn't breathe because she was reading it. I wanted her to turn around and smile at me, but she kept looking straight ahead.

    Mr. Pinkerton asked everybody to clear their desks and get our maps workbooks, which are in a bin on the counter. Everybody got busy, putting away stuff and getting out the workbooks. And in the middle of that, Isabella walked past my desk and dropped a tiny folded note on it.

    My hands were shaky when I opened it. And then I saw the words. "Thanks, Kristin. It's okay," she wrote. "Your friend, Isabella."

I read it over and over. And then the lesson started and I had to look as if I were paying attention so I didn't get in trouble. And even though Mr. Pinkerton said that the only thing that should be on our desks was our map workbook, I kept the note there. I put my left hand over it so I could hide it, and I swear I could feel the words coming up from the paper into my hand. Like the ink was warm.

We are all hoping, hoping, hoping that tomorrow when we walk in the door, Mrs. Penrose is back and the baby is okay and everything is normal.

Important Message from Omar

1. Terrible news this morning. Mr. Pinkerton is still here.

2. "I have been informed that Mrs. Penrose is having a medical emergency," Mr. Pinkerton said. "I will be your teacher for the time being."

3. Isabella whispered, "Omar, what does 'time being' mean?"

4. I whispered, "I don't know."

5. The room was more silent than blank paper.

6. I saw tears start to come out of Isabella's eyes and Tee's eyes, but they blinked them back inside.

7. We did morning work. Then we did afternoon work.

8. I'm writing this after school while I'm waiting for my bus to get called.

9.   We have a lot of questions, and we have
     to wait all weekend! Is Mrs. Penrose
     okay? Is the baby okay? When is she
     coming back?

This is Tee. Everybody let me take home the book and said I could start writing the WOW story in it, but I can't stop worrying.

Come   back
    tomorrow,   M   r   s   .
    Penrose.   Come   back   tomorrow,
    Mrs. Penrose. Come   back tomorrow, Mrs.
    Penrose.   Come   back tomorrow, Mrs. Penrose.
    Come back tomorrow, Mrs. Penrose. Come back
    tomorrow, Mrs. Penrose. Come back tomorrow,
    Mrs. Penrose. Come back tomorrow, Mrs. Penrose.
    Come back tomorrow, Mrs. Penrose. Come back
    tomorrow, Mrs. Penrose. Come back tomorrow,
    Mrs. Penrose. Come back tomorrow, Mrs. Penrose.
    Come back tomorrow, Mrs. Penrose. <u>PLEASE</u>.
    Come back tomorrow, Mrs. Penrose. Come
    back tomorrow, Mrs. Penrose. Come back
    tomorrow, Mrs. Penrose. Come back
    tomorrow, Mrs. Penrose. Come
    back   tomorrow,
    Mrs. Penrose.
    C o m e
    b a c k

MONDAY, DECEMBER 23

Mrs. Penrose is not here again.

This morning Ms. Yang comes into our room.

"Mrs. Penrose sent me an e-mail and she wants me to share it with you," Ms. Yang says. She reads.

Dear Boys and Girls,

This is Mrs. Penrose. I know you are all wondering what is going on. Last Tuesday night, I had to go to the hospital. The baby decided to come early. His name is Ryan. He is tiny and needs help breathing. His lungs aren't ready for the world. He needs to stay in the hospital. I miss you all, but I need to stay here with him for now.

I don't know how long I will be gone.

Please be helpful to your substitute and be good friends to one another. Within each of you is a flame, a passion for learning. Keep the

flame burning brightly by reading and
writing a lot.

Enjoy your holidays and don't
worry about me or the baby. We
are in good hands. I will see you all
sometime in the New Year.

Your teacher,
Mrs. Penrose

When Ms. Yang starts reading, her voice sounds
shaky. Like she's walking on a tightrope and about to fall
off. Then when she gets to the last part, she starts to
cry and her eyes get red all around the edges. I have to
look at my shoelaces because her eyes make me want to
cry. My shoelaces are dirty.

She gives the e-mail to Mr. Pinkerton.

"The baby was supposed to be born in March," Kristin
says.

Ms. Yang nods.

Nobody says anything.

She stands up and smiles, but it's the kind of smile
you do to stop crying. "I'm sure he'll be okay," she says.
Her voice is still shaky.

After lunch, I find the e-mail in the recycle bin by

Mr. pinkerton's desk. I don't think important letters from teachers should be in recycle bins. I secretly take it out and tape it in this book.

I was going to say that I am afraid Mrs. penrose is never coming back, but I am not going to say it. Good things <u>can</u> happen. Mali Koam wrote back. That was a good thing that happened, so a good thing could happen with the baby. When we get back from Winter Break, maybe Mrs. penrose will be sitting at her desk. I hope so. (But I am still scared.)

— Isabella

What exactly are lungs? — Carly

The part of your chest that fills up with air when you breath in.

— Buzz

Everybody should try to have happy holidays even though we are worried.

—Jazmine

This is Alexander H. Gory, Jr., writing at twenty-one minutes after midnight. The New Year is officially here. I am in my bunk bed with my flashlight, a pen and this book. Fat snowflakes are falling outside as if the sky won't ever run out of them.

My brother just fell asleep. They let us stay up to ring in the New Year. Being up late always makes me feel like I'm doing something against the law.

My parents are still downstairs clinking their glasses with our neighbors. The voices of the grown-ups are like another language because I can't understand what they're saying. They sound like elves living under my floor.

I have a confession. Even though the New Year is supposed to be a happy time, and even though it was fun to stay up late, I'm feeling sad because we missed the deadline for the contest, which was December 31st. Yesterday. I'm also feeling guilty because of what happened on the last day of school when we got that letter from Mrs. Penrose. At first I was sad and worried for her and the baby, but then I realized that we were going to miss the deadline for the contest, and I got a little mad at the baby for coming early. I feel terrible about that. A nicer person would just feel sad for the baby, not mad about missing a contest. I know Ryan didn't come early on purpose, and I hereby want to take back my madness at him.

I have another thing to get off my chest. You know how I always want things to be suspenseful? I didn't mean that I want scary things like this to happen. I still want suspense in stories, but in real life right now I want things to be okay. I want to go back to school and find out that the baby is all right. Tomorrow I shall sleep with all my fingers crossed, and I shall try to cross my toes, too, but I'm not sure they will cooperate.

Even though I'm worried about baby Ryan, I'm also really disappointed about the contest. I wanted to win. I feel bad about saying that at a time like this, but it's the truth and nothing but the truth. And that makes me feel ~~badder~~ worse.

— Carly

The First Day Back

by Kristin

What Alexander wrote was brave. I was feeling guilty because the same thought crossed my mind for a split second. Why did that baby have to come early and mess up our story-writing project! And then I felt terrible.

Anyway, we walked in with our fingers crossed. But there was Mr. Pinkerton.

Nobody said anything out loud about it because we were too sad. Then Harrison said, "The air is so cold today, it makes my lungs hurt." And that made me think about baby Ryan and his lungs, and I could tell everybody else was thinking about him, too.

The temperature is 11 degrees Fahrenheit and the windchill is minus 10. As my mom says, today is a day that could freeze the bark out of a dog, which means indoor recess with Mr. Pinkerton.

Mr. Pinkerton gave us three choices for indoor recess: play a board game quietly with a friend, read, or catch up on any work we didn't finish. He didn't say write, but he didn't say no writing. I'm in the Good Book Nook writing in this book. Tee is over here now, and she's whispering that she wants to write something, so hold on.

I wanted to say a thank-you to Isabella for rescuing the letter from the recycle bin and taping it in here. It helps to read what Mrs. Penrose wrote. This is the saddest time of my life. I cannot stop thinking about baby Ryan. I've been worried because it's so cold outside, which means they can't have any windows open and maybe his lungs need fresh air.

Love,
Tee

My mom says milk makes bones grow. Can't there be some food we can give to baby Ryan to make his lungs grow? I'm going to pass this book around and we can all write down our ideas.

—Kristen

Yo, maybe fizzy stuff would work? All those bubbles fill up your insides with air and make you burp.

— Nick

This is not a funny time, Nick.

—Jazmine

Actually, I wasn't trying to be funny.
— Nick

I think the baby is probably getting oxygen through a tube or a mask. My grandpa had that.

—Harrison

In the movies they breathe into somebody's mouth to make the oxygen go in. Maybe they should try that, not just once, but every day until his lungs are bigger. Tee is right, this is the saddest time.

—Carly

I just want that little baby to be all better.

—Isabella

Maybe Mrs. Penrose could bring Ryan to school and we could all take turns breathing fresh air on him.

—Jazmine

People don't make oxygen. People make carbon dioxide. So I don't think breathing on him would help. But plants make oxygen. Remember the leaf experiment we did? When we cut our leaves and put them in those cups of water and left them in the sunlight, all those little bubbles appeared in the water. That was because the leaf was making oxygen from the sunlight. They make oxygen all the time. We just don't usually see it. We could surround his little crib with plants. The walls could be crawling with vines!

Signed, Alexander H. Gory, Jr.

To the Whole Class,

1. Remember that the longer we let the plants sit in the sunlight, the more bubbles.

2. Maybe Ryan just needs time and then little by little he'll be okay.

3. This is also reminding me of the thing my dad has by our fireplace. It is called a bellows. He says fires need oxygen in order to live. When the fire starts to

die out, he blows air on it with the
bellows and then the wood starts
to glow red and then pretty soon a little
flame leaps out and the fire
starts again.

4. Maybe we could tell the doctors about
    the bellows and they could make
    an invention like it to help.

Sincerely,
Omar

I hope baby Ryan is in a really big room with lots
of plants and lots of sunshine. Recess is over, but
let's all write more tomorrow.

—Tee

Something bad happened yesterday with this book, and it's my fault. Here's what happened.

I couldn't wait until recess to write, so during math I went to the Good Book Nook to get a tissue and slipped this book under my shirt while Mr. Pinkerton was plugging in the projector.

Nick saw me and waved at me to pass the book to him. I passed the book to Omar because he sits between me and Nick. Omar nervously threw the book back at me, but it landed on Tee's desk with a <u>thunk</u> because she sits behind me.

Mr. Pinkerton saw it. "What's going on, Tee?" He walked over and picked up our book. "We're doing math right now. Is this your math book?"

Tee was too scared to even talk.

Nick said very loudly, "It's my—"

"I didn't ask for a comment from you, Nick," Mr. Pinkerton said.

Then Harrison tried. "He was just trying to—"

Mr. Pinkerton held up his hand. "Enough. Right now we're doing math. Period." He put our book on his desk.

Carly raised her hand.

"Is your question related to math?"

"No," Carly said, and put her hand down.

At recess, we all met by the pine tree. Everybody was mad at me for getting the book and at Omar for throwing it and at Mr. Pinkerton for being so mean.

"I've had it with Mr. Finkerton," Carly said. "I'm going to demand that he give the book back."

"Don't make him mad," Isabella said.

"CBC," Jazmine said. "Compliment before criticism."

"I'll be charming," Carly said.

When we went back to the room, she marched right up to Mr. Pinkerton and smiled. "We all like your glasses, Mr. Pinkerton," she said.

"Thank you." He looked confused. I don't think he gets a lot of compliments.

"You know that?" Carly pointed to our book. "We were just wondering if you could put it back in the Good Book Nook. We would like very much to write in it when our work is done and during indoor recess and after school while we're waiting for the bus. We use it to practice our spelling and many other educational things."

He picked up the book. "You can write in it on

Fridays at the end of the day if you have your work done," he said. "But I'm keeping it here." He opened Mrs. Penrose's desk drawer and dropped it in.

That's it. One lousy day a week.

Today is Friday. I got my work done so I could ask for the book. Other people want to write in this book, but the bell is about to ring. I'm sorry that I took up all the writing time, but if I didn't get this off my chest I would explode into a million bits.

Farewell,

Alexander H. Gory, Jr.

Carly just walked around and silently gave everybody (except for Mr. Pinkerton, of course) a friendship wristband for free. We all put them on. We are united. Thank you, Carly. (I really wanted one, but I didn't have the money.)

The Very Bright Writers of Delite vs.
Mr. Finkersnot

A WOW Story by Slick

At Delite Elementary School, there was a classroom full of very bright writers who wanted to write in their book. But a grumpy substitute named Mr. Finkersnot took the book away.

One frosty day, the students had a meeting by the old pine tree.

"How can we get rid of Mr. Finkersnot?" a girl named Krusty asked.

"I have a friend who can help," a boy named Elaxander said. Then he closed his eyes and whispered, "Come here now," in a spooky voice.

A boy ghost appeared.

A student named Izzybelly screamed.

"Never fear," said Elaxander. "This ghost isn't here to haunt us. He's my friend."

"Yep," said the boy ghost. "My name is Bob."

A most excellent dude named Slick asked, "So, how did you kick the bucket, Bob?"

"I was a student in Mr. Finkersnot's class last year," Bob said. "I died of boredom. So, what do you want from me today?"

"We want to get rid of Mr. Finkersnot," Harryson said.

"Yeah," Buzzard said. "Can you help?"

"Abso-dabbo-lutely," Bob said.

The students cheered. They wanted to lift him up on their shoulders, but he just slipped through their fingers.

"Meet me at Mr. Finkersnot's house at midnight," Bob said, and floated away like a cloud.

That night all the students met outside Mr. Finkersnot's house. Bob had a special ghost dust that he sprinkled on them to make them all invisible for exactly one hour. Then they went into the house.

Mr. Finkersnot was already asleep. His shirt and pants for the morning were all laid out on top of his dresser. He was giving the students in his class a six-hour test the next day, and he wanted to get there early to sharpen all the pencils.

The invisible students went to work.

Elaxander and Slick put Mr. Finkersnot's alarm clock in the refrigerator. Izzybelly, Jazzy, Teacup and Narly put bright orange dye in his shampoo. Buzzard, Omart and Harryson took out all the lightbulbs and hid them in the closet. And, last but not least, Krusty took the feathers out of a pillow and glued them all over his shirt and pants.

Then they slipped through the walls, went back to their houses and got into their own beds before the ghost dust wore off.

Bob floated away silently. His job helping the Writers of Delite was done.

In the morning the kids went to school. They were lined up on the playground waiting to go in. The principal looked angry. "Where is Mr. Finkersnot? He is late."

Just then the students saw a giant chicken running across the field toward the school.

"I'm here! I'm here!" the giant chicken yelled. "My alarm didn't go off and the lights in my house wouldn't go on. I had to take a shower and get dressed in the dark. But I'm here!"

"Mr. Finkersnot!" the principal exclaimed. He had bright orange hair, and white feathers all over his clothes.

"This is not what I expect from my teachers here at Delite Elementary School," the principal told him. "You're fired."

All the students were happy. Mr. Finkersnot was confused. He didn't understand why he was fired. Then he went home, looked in the mirror and fainted with a <u>thunk</u>.

Eventually the poor chap did get a job at the Minnesota Zoo doing the chicken dance on Cluck Like a Chicken Day.

The End

LOL!!!

Great story!

Ha ha ha ha ha ha ha for real!

Hilarious!

Dear Mrs. Penrose,

I am taping this letter in this book so that you will see it when you come back. It explains why I will not allow the students to write in this book anymore.

At first, I agreed to allow students to write on Fridays if they finished all their work. Last Friday, Nick did not complete his math, spelling or history. He did manage to find time to write a story about a "Mr. Finkersnot."

I discovered it today.

The story was completely inappropriate. I told the students that I was taking away the book. I also explained we will be taking the state Path to Success tests soon, and, according to the school calendar, all attention should be focused on getting ready for them.

Sincerely,
Mr. Pinkerton

Nick's Surprise

by Kristin

Our class is on the road to being criminals. We have stolen this book back! Here's the scoop.

At recess, Nick and Buzz told everybody to meet down by the pine tree.

When we were all there, Nick said, "Hey, guys, look what we have."

Buzz lifted up his shirt. The class book was tucked inside his pants.

Omar had a fit.

We all said ssshhh.

"How did you get that?" Isabella asked.

"We made a cover that looks like our book cover and put it over Mali Koam's 'Secret Pages.' It looks just like our book! When Mr. Pinkerton wasn't looking, we switched the books."

"But Mrs. Penrose specifically told us to be helpful to the substitute," Omar whispered. "Stealing is not helpful."

"This book belongs to us. He's the one who stole it from us," Buzz said.

"We'll get caught," Isabella said.

"Who cares? Nobody likes Mr. Pinkerton," Carly said.

"I feel sorry for him," Omar said.

"Do you like him?" Carly asked.

"No," Omar said. "But he's just trying to do his job. Mrs. Penrose would want us to be good students."

"Mrs. Penrose also told us to keep the flame of passion burning," Harrison said.

There was a moment of silence.

"Harrison speaks the truth," Alexander said.

Harrison smiled.

Alexander went on. "Mrs. Penrose told us to read and write a lot. And our class book inspires us to do that. Mr. Pinkerton probably only read Nick's story. He probably didn't read the whole book. It's like judging a book by its cover. He thinks the whole book is inappropriate. That's wrong."

"I think we should return the book to Mr. Pinkerton before he finds out," Omar said.

"We'll get caught trying," Isabella said.

"We could put this book back and just get a new blank book," Omar said.

"That wouldn't be the same. I love going back and reading all the letters," Tee said. "Just seeing all the writing in our book makes my brain on fire to write."

"We could write to Mrs. Penrose and ask her what to do," Omar said.

Tee almost started to cry. "What if she is ashamed of us?"

"Let's write to Mali Koam for advice," Harrison said.

Once again, the shy guy makes the touchdown.

Dear Mali Koam,

Our real teacher is in the hospital because her baby's lungs aren't ready for the world. We are worried. On top of that, our substitute doesn't like our collaborative book. He hid it in his drawer.

We got crabby and desperate for our book. My mom gets like this when she is out of coffee.

We stole it back.

Here's the thing. Someone in our class wrote a WOW story about the substitute. The whole thing hurt Mr. Pinkerton's feelings. Mr. Pinkerton is boring, but you're not supposed to say that to someone in the face. If Mrs. Penrose were here, this wouldn't have happened.

By the way, the story had a want, an obstacle, and a win. We learned a lot from you.

It's recess right now. We are all sitting down by the pine tree, and we don't know what to do. We are going to mail this letter tonight. We hope you write back. I (Kristin) will put in a stamped envelope with my address on it so you can send me a letter back to my house.

Truly yours,
The Writers of Delite

P.S. It's too dangerous to write in this book and it's too dangerous to return it. So until we figure out what to do, Alexander is hiding it in his cubby.

This is Alexander. By the way, since you live in Maryland I will tell you that I went to a famous graveyard once in Baltimore, Maryland. It was delightfully spooky. Farewell.

A letter came from Maryland!

I am taping it here and showing everybody at recess today.

— FROM THE DESK OF MALI KOAM —

Dear Writers of Delite,

Oh dear. Sounds like you have a lot of complex issues. I wanted to write back right away.

I am so sorry about Mrs. Penrose and hope that her baby is all right. I'm sure that the doctors and nurses at the hospital are taking good care of both of them.

I can tell that you value your class book. I love the way you wrote that you became "crabby and desperate" when you couldn't write. We are kindred spirits, indeed. Stories are like oxygen to me.

My guess is that the story about the substitute was funny but also hurtful. That's the thing about writing. Words are powerful. They can heal us or they can hurt us.

Has the author of the story written a letter of apology to Mr. Pinkerton? A letter can often express what is difficult to say. Letters also allow the reader time to reread and think over the matter. That sometimes helps.

Can you find a way to channel your creative energy in a positive direction? Can you find a way for your stories to be funny without hurting anyone's feelings? Can you write stories that heal instead of hurt?

Yours truly,

Mali Koam

Every once in a while, you have an extraordinary day. The sky is bluer for you. The sun is warmer for you. The air is filled with electricity.

We, the Writers of Delite, are having an extraordinary day. The letter we got from Mali Koam filled us all with secret energy. It's lunch right now and I'm too jumpy to write, so I'm going to hand this over to Kristin. She'll write down what happened.

— Alexander H. Gory, Jr.

The Plan

by Kristin

At recess we all raced down to our meeting spot and read the letter three times in a row.

"Mali Koam says that stories are like oxygen," Tee said. "We should write that WOW story for Mrs. Penrose and give it to her so that she can read it to baby Ryan. Stories heal." She was so excited she was bouncing on the tips of her toes like a balloon trying to float up.

"Words can't really heal anything, only medicine can do that," Omar said quickly.

All the air went out of Tee, and out of the rest of us, too.

Harrison stepped up onto the merry-go-round. "I respectfully disagree with Omar," he said. We all looked at him. "Words can make you feel better. When Alexander wrote that he liked my story idea about touching the moon and that he liked my letter to Mali Koam, those were all just words. But his words made me feel better. Maybe words aren't miracles like abracadabra, you're all better, but words can give you a good feeling that helps you when things are hard, like when you move to someplace new and nobody likes you at first. That's a kind of healing."

We were all quiet for a moment.

Alexander nodded. "I agree. I think when words are written down, they get even stronger power."

I agree, too. I remembered how good it felt to write the "I'm sorry" note to Isabella and how her note made me get unfrozen.

"I like words in very black ink because the ink is so black and the page is so white and you can read those words over and over anytime you want," Tee said.

"Let's do Tee's rabbit story," Jazmine said. "It'll be a great present for the baby. Mrs. Penrose will love it. She said she wanted to read it, remember? Let's all take turns."

"Tee gets to start and finish," I said. "The rest of us will write when it's our turn."

"You know, if our story is good we could give it to the baby <u>and</u> sell it for a million bucks," Carly added. "Just saying."

"Nick should write a letter of apology to Mr. Pinkerton like Mali Koam suggested," Omar said. "And we have to explain about swapping out the books. It will be better for us to tell him than for him to find out."

"I think we should all write the letter together," I said. "It can be an apology letter, but it can also be a persuasive, informative letter. We can get him to change his mind about the book."

"Let's put the letter in this book and deliver it to him

with the page marked 'Read This, Please,'" Alexander said. "We'll ask him to write his reply in the book. That way we'll have a record of the whole thing."

"Alexander can add some nice pictures to Nick's letter, maybe one showing Mr. Pinkerton looking handsome," Jazmine said. "That could help."

Carly stood up. "We have a plan. Let's write the apology first. That's a wrap."

"When it's time to write the story, I hope I can think of how to start," Tee said.

"Don't stare at the blank page," Harrison said. "Close your eyes and really picture your main character like Mali Koam does. Where is the rabbit? What is he doing? What is he thinking? Then open your eyes and write."

"Go big or go home," Buzz said.

Omar let out a breath. "I hope Mr. Pinkerton forgives and forgets."

"He will," Isabella said. We all looked at her and she shrugged. "We're good writers. After he reads our letter, it will be okay."

Recess is over. Our plan begins on Monday.

Dear Mr. Pinkerton,

As you can see, we stole the book back. Actually, I (Nick) took this book and put a different one in its place. We were desperate. I'm sorry about that and about the Mr. Finkersnot story. I was trying to be funny, but I didn't think about how you would feel if you saw it. I get carried away sometimes like Nick. I'm sorry, too. Please read this book starting at the beginning so you can see what it's all about. But you do not need to read the Mr. Finkersnot story again, because that might make you mad again. We would like to write a story for Mrs. Penrose and her baby and send it to her. We will only work on this during recess. We will not fight about who will write in it next or what we will write, because we have all agreed. Please, please say yes. Even though writing this story is not on the state test, and it will not make us rich, we are learning something valuable, and my spelling is getting better and better. **It is making even me want to write (I'm Buzz).**

Respectfully yours,
The Writers of Delite

P.S. Please write your reply in this book.

Dear Class,

I read your letter, and I decided to read the rest
of your book. I can see that there are many educational
things about it. I will allow you to write in the class book
during recess. As I said before, you may also write in it on
Fridays if you are done with your work. The book will stay
on my desk when it is not in use. Please respect my rules,
and I will respect your desire to write in the book.

Sincerely,
Mr. Pinkerton

Great news! We can keep writing. Hurray!!!! Tee gets to start. Remember, this is just our rough draft. Don't take forever. Just get something down and pass it on.

We can always make it better.

The Tiny Rabbit

by the Writers of Delite

A rabbit was born in a warm, cozy house. He was just a tiny thing.

One night his mother told him that winter was almost over. She said when he got stronger she would take him down the hill. Other rabbits lived there and they would be his friends.

He couldn't stop thinking about those other rabbits. He really wanted to hop out and find them. One night, when everyone was fast asleep, he decided to do it.

At midnight, the little rabbit hopped up to the surface.

The prairie was under a white quilt of snow. On one side of the hill was a creek. Here and there, pine trees were holding out their branches. In the black sky, the moon was hanging just over the top of the hill, surrounded by stars.

The rabbit jumped for joy. He thought the moon and stars were other rabbits.

He went to find them. He kept hopping through the night.

As he hopped, he didn't notice that the sky was changing. Heavy clouds came and crowded the sky. The wind picked up its speed. It howled through the leaves of the trees. Suddenly, a bad mix of sleet and freezing rain came down.

Boom! Crack! Lightning and thunder. A terrifying winter storm. The tiny, helpless rabbit shivered in fear.

Things got worse for the poor guy.

He called out, "Mama!" But he was too far from home.

He turned to hop back, but he slipped on an icy patch and slid down, down, down. He landed with a terrible splash in that cold creek.

He holds his breath and tries to feel for the ground with his feet, but the water is too deep and moving too fast.

The rushing creek carries him along. Luckily, a stick floats by and he reaches out and grabs it. He floats along. He keeps his head above water.

He saw his own house. The rushing creek was carrying him past his own house!

"Help!" the bunny called out as he held on to the stick and paddled to keep his head above the water.

But his parents were underground, still fast asleep.

"Wake up, sleepyheads!" the rabbit yelled. "Can't a bunny get a break around here?"

Nope. The bunny was swept right past his house.

The sleet and freezing rain stopped
and the sun came out, and so things
got better for the bunny. Still, he was
floating along, and he really didn't know
how he was going to get out of that creek.

But he smiled and said to himself,
"Something good will happen."

Down the hill, there was another house with ten
rabbits just like his mother said. They happened to hear
the rabbit crying out for help.

"We have to do something," one of the other rabbits
said.

They quickly found a rope and threw it across the
creek.

As the little rabbit was swept closer, they yelled out to
him. "Grab the rope and we'll pull you in."

The little rabbit reached up with his paw and grabbed the rope.

The others pulled him in. The rabbit climbed out of the water. The ground felt firm underneath his feet.

"Thank you very much for the rescue," the rabbit said.

Just then, the mother rabbit came hopping up. When she woke up and saw that her bunny was gone, she had been very worried. She had been searching for him everywhere.

"I was so worried, but you're okay," she said, and hugged him.

Being in that water had scared him, but he made it.

"You must be hungry," she said, and gave him a carrot.

He got to play with his friends and lived happily ever after.

The End

To the Whole Class:

1. Our story is good, but we can make it much better.
2. I'm doing some research on rabbits to find more facts about them. Their underground homes are called warrens, and they make tunnels in a zigzag pattern to keep predators from finding them easily. That's just two facts we can add to the story. I have more.
3. I am going to ask Mr. Pinkerton if we can spend time talking about how we can improve it. We'll compliment before criticizing.

Sincerely,
Omar

Hi,

I like our story, but I agree with Omar.
Let's give the characters names, and
make their character traits stronger. If
the rabbit is really young, he wouldn't
know much about the world or even how
to talk. That could be interesting.

—Harrison

P.S. Omar, that means when the rabbit
talks, he will make mistakes. Don't
correct those.

Greetings Fellow Fiction Writers,

I have a HUGE IDEA to make the story better.
I am jumping inside because it's so great. I got this
idea while I was walking to the bus stop. Mali Koam
is right about how walking can give you ideas.
It's an idea for a new character to add suspense
and another obstacle to the story. When I told Mr.
Pinkerton about it this morning, he smiled and said,
"Nick, Kristin, Tee and Buzz just told me their ideas.
You are all on fire."

He told me that we can take class time tomorrow and tell him all our suggestions. He'll write them on the smartboard. Then we can work on making our changes every day until we get to THE END. That's what he said, "every day," not just on Fridays.

Burning with excitement,
Alexander H. Gory, Jr.

I got some ideas, too. Bunny baby, we are going to go big or go home on you.

— Buzz

Our Revision

by Kristin

Well, as my mom says, good cooking takes time.
We worked on our story every day for over two weeks.
We corrected all our mistakes. It's the longest and best
thing we've ever done. Mr. Pinkerton made three copies:
one for us to put in this book, one for us to send to Mrs.
Penrose, and one for us to send to Mali Koam.

Everybody should read it again. Tomorrow, let's write
a card to go with it. Okay, drumroll, please . . .

Riggy Pepper

by the Writers of Delite

CHAPTER 1

Underneath the snow, Riggy Pepper was born in a warm, cozy warren. At first, he was just a tiny thing with brown fur, a white tail and a pink nose. He couldn't even hop. Every night, his mother told him a story, gave him a hug and tucked him in.

One night Mrs. Pepper said, "Winter is almost over, Riggy. Soon, when you are stronger, we will hop down the hill. Other rabbits live there, and they'll be your friends. You can play with them."

"Me wanna go now," Riggy said, jumping out of bed. "Me strong. See? Big foot!" He tried to hold up one foot, but he lost his balance and fell down.

"Oh, Riggy." His mother smiled. "Have patience. The world is a dangerous place, and you are still too little."

Riggy couldn't stop thinking about those other rabbits. One night, when his mother and father were deep in dreams of cabbages and carrots, he decided to find his friends.

CHAPTER 2

Excited, Riggy followed their tunnel up through the dark earth as it zigzagged toward the surface. Suddenly his nose pressed against something cold and wet. Snow! Of course, he didn't know what it was. To him, it was a cold, wet wall. He pushed his nose into it again, breathing hard, and his breath melted a little of it.

He dug into it with his front paws, making a small snowball. He licked it.

Yum!

"Me like this wall," Riggy said to himself. Little by little, he dug and munched and ate his way through the snow that was blocking part of their hole. Then his head poked out into the fresh air of the cold, dark night.

The rolling hill of the prairie was tucked in tight under a white quilt of snow. On one side of the hill trickled the cold water of a creek. Here and there, pine trees were holding their branches out to the sky.

Riggy sat very still, catching his

breath, looking at the perfect snow, listening to the music of the creek, and feeling the fingertips of the wind on his fur. Then he turned and looked up. In the black sky, the full round moon was hanging just over the top of the hill, surrounded by white shining stars.

Riggy jumped for joy. He thought the moon and stars were other rabbits.

"That be the mama rabbit and all my friends. They no sleeping. They be waiting for me." He began to hop up the hill. "Me coming! Me wanna play!"

Up he went. His small hops left tracks in the snow. Soon Riggy was getting tired, but he was a determined little guy, and he kept hopping through the night. He was building up his bunny muscles.

CHAPTER 3

Way at the top of the hill, an owl was perched in a pine tree. He was a very proper owl with a round, white face and frightening yellow eyes that never seemed to blink. He turned his head and saw a set of shadow tracks below.

"Interesting," he said to himself. The tracks were

slowly, slowly moving up the hill. He lifted off his branch and sailed down for a closer look. "Ah . . . a delicious-looking mammal. I have already eaten my dinner, but I do so love a plump, juicy bunny for dessert."

He swooped down silently with his sharp talons sticking out.

The tiny rabbit did not suspect a thing. He was hopping along when suddenly the owl grabbed him by the scruff of his neck and lifted him off the ground.

"Now that I have this prey in my grasp, my stomach is rumbling," said the owl. "I am looking forward to this midnight snack."

His powerful wings sliced through the dark night as he headed to his lair in the ancient, craggy pine tree.

Riggy didn't know what was going on. He just knew he was flying through the air, heading straight for the moon.

He looked up at the owl. "Hey, thanks for the lift. Me tired."

The owl almost dropped him in shock. "You can't thank me. My victims are always terrified of me." He added an evil laugh, just to seal the deal. "Mwa-ha-ha."

As they flew toward the tree, Riggy looked at the snow-covered hill and the creek below. "Wee! Me fly like the wind. Higher! Higher!"

The owl glided along, scowling.

After a moment, Riggy said, "Me Riggy."

"My name is Professor Perchkin the Predator," the owl said with great dignity.

Riggy laughed. "Hi, Buddy."

"I am called Professor Perchkin the Predator," the owl repeated.

"Okay, Buddy!" Riggy started to do a little dance in the air with his hind feet and his front paws. "Me like the wind in my toes. Me like the wind up my nose," he sang. "Sing with me, Buddy."

"That is an extremely silly song," the owl muttered.

"Mama sings with me."

"I'm <u>not</u> your mother."

The rabbit turned his head to try to see his home. Instead, he saw his white tail for the first time. "Hey, Buddy! Me gots a snowball stuck on me."

Professor Perchkin almost had to laugh.

"You are a cottontail rabbit. That is your tail. You are one of the lagomorph species in the genus Sylvilagus."

Riggy wiggled his rear end and laughed. When he turned his head back around, they were about to crash into the tree. "Hey, watch out!" Riggy cried, as the tree came closer and closer. Suddenly the owl let go, dropping him into the owl's nest. A moment later, Professor Perchkin landed next to him on the branch.

Riggy looked into the owl's round face and then at the moon just beyond him. "Hey, me wanna go there and play."

"You are my prey," the owl said, "and this is my domain."

"Aw, you wanna play, too?" Riggy started dancing in the nest.

"I do not play. I eat," said the owl.

"Me eat, too," Riggy said. He hopped over to the tree trunk and licked it. "Yuck!" He picked up a paw full of snow and ate a mouthful. "Yum!" He held it out to Professor Perchkin and smiled. "You wanna eat, Buddy?"

The owl blinked. He had never captured prey quite like Riggy, and it was throwing him off. He closed his eyes for a moment, wondering what to do. When . . . smack!

The little guy threw a snowball at him. "Play! Play!" Riggy jumped up and down on the branch.

Professor Perchkin laughed. "As my dear mother always says, 'If you can't beat 'em, join 'em!' "

They had a major snowball fight.

Chapter 4

After they were done, Professor Perchkin shook the snow from his wings and said, "Who am I trying to fool? I can't eat you, Riggy." Gently he picked up Riggy, flew down, and set him on the snow. "Burrow underneath the snow and get some rest. In the morning, you can hop home."

The little rabbit looked up at the owl. "Nighty-night." He held out his arms for a hug.

Professor Perchkin cleared his throat. "Um . . . um . . . owls do not give good-night hugs—" Before he could finish, Riggy jumped forward and gave him a big hug.

"Oh for heaven's sake," Professor Perchkin said, patting the rabbit on the head with the tip of his wing. "Now go to sleepy—I mean, go to sleep, Riggy."

The little rabbit dug a hole under the snow and fell fast asleep.

The owl waited until he heard him snoring, and then he flew back up to this nest.

"What a strange night," he said to himself as he looked out over the hillside.

Finally the owl tucked his head down and fell asleep. The moon and stars closed their eyes and floated off, too. While everyone was sleeping, the sun was waking up. She wanted to put on her new yellow dress and strut her stuff, but some clouds had big plans. Like a bunch of bullies, they crowded the sky. When morning came they started storming, sending down a bad mix of sleet and freezing rain. The wind picked up its speed. Like a wild wolf, it howled through the leaves of the trees.

Chapter 5

Riggy's mother woke up to find Riggy missing. "Wake up!" Mrs. Pepper said to her husband. "Riggy is gone." They looked in all the tunnels, but he wasn't there. Finally his mother hurried all the way up to the surface and looked out.

A storm! Sleet and rain!

The mother rabbit froze in fear, her fur ruffling in the wind.

Boom! Crack! Lightning and thunder!

She jumped. "Riggy! Where are you?" She shivered and began hopping all around. "Riggy? Come back! Come back!"

She was hoping that her bunny would hear her voice.

Plink! Plink! The freezing rain hit the snow above Riggy's face and woke him up. He dug his way out of his little burrow in the snow. It wasn't night, but the sky was dark.

Far away from his warren, he called out, "Mama!" Only the wind howled back. Scared, he turned to hop back home, but he slipped on an icy patch and slid. He landed with a terrible splash in the creek.

The bunny had never been in water and didn't know what to do. The water was cold and rushing. He held his breath and tried to feel for the ground with his feet, but the water was too deep and moving too fast.

Down the hill the creek rushed, carrying poor Riggy in its watery arms. His tiny lungs felt empty and tight. His last bits of oxygen were disappearing. Desperately he paddled up to the surface and gasped for air.

His legs and arms were growing tired. He didn't know if he could make it. Just then, a stick floated by and he reached out and grabbed it.

The rushing creek was carrying Riggy right past his own warren. His mother and father were there. He could see them.

"Help! Help!" the bunny called out as he held on to the stick and paddled to keep his head above the water.

Mr. and Mrs. Pepper were searching for him, but their backs were to the creek, and the sound of the wind was filling their ears.

"If I can just yell louder," the bunny thought. He struggled to take a deeper breath, but his lungs were so small. "Help! Help!"

As the bunny was swept away by the water, the sound of his cry was swept away by the wind.

Chapter 6

Poor Riggy struggled in the cold water, trying to paddle over to the side. But the current of the creek kept pulling him along.

Ahead, he saw a branch that had fallen across the creek. If only he could grab onto that, then he could climb out of the creek.

As he passed under it, he took a chance. He let go of his stick and reached up. His left paw slipped, but his right paw grabbed hold of the branch. The problem was that he didn't have enough strength left to pull himself out of the water.

Desperately, he tried to reach up with his feet.

Although Riggy didn't know it, his movement caught the attention of two creatures who happened to be out.

Nickers and Abbit, two rabbits from the warren at the bottom of the hill, were on duty that day. They were hiding under a bush. It was their job to watch for predators.

"Check that out," Nickers said. "A sewer rat is stuck on that branch in the creek."

"What's he doing so far from the big city?" Abbit wondered.

Krikri and Higgin popped out of the warren hole and looked.

"That's not a sewer rat," Krikri said.

"That's a rabbit!" Higgin said. "That's one of us."

Quickly they thumped their feet, sending a signal to the warren below.

Six other rabbits came up. They were all good friends. You could tell because they were all wearing friendship bands around their front paws that a rabbit named Cuffy had made.

"That rabbit is going to lose his hold," said Tippy.

"Or the branch will break," said Innzy.

"We need to help," Jaja said.

"Time for action," Buff agreed.

Quickly they began to hop toward the creek.

Chapter 7

At that same moment, Professor Perchkin opened his eyes.

"Ah, I see the weather has taken a rather nasty turn," he said to himself. "I think I'll stay in my tree." He wrapped his wings around himself like a cape, and then he spied Riggy struggling to hold on to the branch. "That little whippersnapper doesn't know how to swim. He'll drown!" He shook his head. "This is none of my business. I will not get involved." He tried to look away, but couldn't. "Oh pish posh, I have to do something!" He lifted off from the branch and headed out to help.

The owl was focused on Riggy. He liked Riggy and was thinking about him and nothing but him. That was why he didn't notice all the other rabbits heading for the creek.

Unfortunately, the other rabbits didn't know he was on Riggy's side. It was their natural instinct to be afraid of the owl.

"Enemy!" Odar cried. "We have to scare him away."

Chapter 8

Nickers, Abbit, Buff and Cuffy stopped right before the fallen branch. They made hard iceballs with their paws. The others quickly followed.

Riggy looked up and saw Professor Perchkin swooping down.

"Hurray!" Riggy thought. He couldn't hold on to the branch another moment.

Just then, the rabbits threw the iceballs. One whizzed by the owl's face, another by his back, and then another, and another. Dazed, Professor Perchkin darted up and swerved away.

"No!" Riggy cried, and let go of the branch. He fell into the cold water.

The rabbits quickly held hands to make a chain and jumped into the creek. The fast current made Riggy slam up against their linked arms, but they didn't let the chain break. Riggy used the last of his strength to reach out with his paws. He grabbed hold of one of the friendship bands.

The rabbits cheered.

"Hold on! We'll pull you in," Tippy said.

They pulled him safely to the bank of the creek. Riggy could feel his feet on the ground again. He hopped onto the field and collapsed. He was so tired, he could hardly breathe. His fur was completely wet. His ears were droopy, and his tail was stringy.

"Are you sure this dude is a rabbit?" Nickers asked.

"He really does look like a sewer rat," Higgin added.

Riggy tried to lift his head to see if Professor Perchkin was okay. "Buddy," he gasped.

"The owl is your buddy?" Krikri asked.

"Look," Jaja said. Professor Perchkin was on the other side of the river, watching them with his yellow, unblinking eyes.

"The little fellow's name is Riggy," Professor Perchkin said. "He's a friend."

"Sorry about those iceballs," Nickers said.

Professor Perchkin shrugged his feathery shoulders. "You were just doing your job."

Riggy smiled, but then his head fell back down to the ground.

Worried, the rabbits and Professor Perchkin huddled around him. They made a bed of soft green pine needles and a canopy of green pine branches in a circle around him. He was breathing, but not as much as he should. They watched over him. All through the day and night, they sang to him and told him stories, even though they didn't know if he could hear them. He wouldn't open his eyes.

Chapter 9

The next morning, the sun came out.
The clouds grumbled away, and the sky
turned blue. Rays of sun warmed up the
pine branches and made a circle of light
on Riggy. The green pine needles grabbed
onto the light and sent out oxygen.

Still, the tiny white fur on Riggy's
chest was hardly moving, and his eyes
stayed closed.

They didn't know what to do.

"Riggy!" a voice called. The rabbits
turned to see Mrs. Pepper hopping down
the hill.

"He's here," Higgin called out.

The other rabbits made a space for
her in the huddle, and Professor Perchkin
stepped back so that he wouldn't
frighten her.

She looked at Riggy and gasped. "Is he
. . . is he all right?" she asked.

They all stood closer, looking down at
the little bunny.

Mrs. Pepper was exhausted. She and
Riggy's father had been searching in

different directions all through the night.
She started to cry. "Oh, Riggy."

The rabbits loved Mrs. Pepper. Before
she had Riggy, she would hop down the
hill and visit them every day. The sound
of her crying was the saddest thing they
had ever heard. They wanted to help her,
but they didn't know how.

Finally she looked at all the rabbits,
with tears shining in her eyes. "Maybe if
we huddle together and focus . . ." Mrs.
Pepper said.

She put her paw softly on Riggy's
chest. One by one the other rabbits put
their paws softly on top of hers.

"What do we want?" Mrs. Pepper
asked.

"We want Riggy to get better," the
friends said, with just the right amount
of energy.

Tears were pouring down Mrs.
Pepper's face. She could hardly speak.
"When do we want it?" she asked.

"Now," the rabbits said.

Gently they lifted their paws up all at
once. The movement made a little <u>whoosh</u>

of air. No one could see it, but the air swirled around and Riggy breathed it in.

"Let's do it again," Higgin said.

Another <u>whoosh</u> of air went into Riggy's lungs.

On the third time, Riggy's eyelids fluttered open.

Chapter 10

"Riggy!" Mrs. Pepper exclaimed.

He looked up and saw his mother and all of his friends in a huddle around him. Behind all their faces, the sky was bright blue.

"Me hungry!" he said.

The rabbits laughed, and Mrs. Pepper hugged him.

"I was so worried, but you're okay," she said, wiping tears away with the back of her paw.

Riggy took another deep breath of delicious air. He was still tired and his muscles were sore, but he could feel the oxygen filling up his lungs and making him stronger and stronger.

He got up and hugged all the rabbits and then he reached out to hug Professor Perchkin.

Noticing the owl for the first time, Mrs. Pepper screamed, "NO!" She jumped to protect Riggy. The owl quickly explained that he was a friend, too.

"Pleased to meet you," Professor Perchkin said. "You have a remarkable son."

"Thank you," Mrs. Pepper said, relieved. She turned to Riggy and said, "Well, that was quite an adventure. I think it's time to go home. Don't you?"

Riggy looked at her with his dark, round eyes. "Me wanna play!"

Mrs. Pepper laughed.

Cuffy gave Riggy a friendship band. It was a little too big for his front paw, so they put it on his hind foot.

He lifted it up. "See? Big foot!"

"Huge foot!" Mrs. Pepper said.

Riggy smiled and looked at all his friends. "Come on, guys. Let's play."

And for the rest of that day, and the rest of his life, Riggy Pepper was a safe and happy little rabbit.

The End

I love our story. Mr. Pinkerton said we
can write our card for Mrs. Penrose today.
Tomorrow, he'll mail it with the story.
On Thursday, we can do the one to Mali
Koam. Hurray!

—Jazmine

Can I start this time?— Omar

Dear Mrs. Penrose,

We miss you. We miss the way your voice sounds like a piano playing when you say good morning.

We miss the Touchdown Twist and the Muddle Huddle.

We miss how you say, "Would you like to phone a friend?" when one of us doesn't know an answer to a question, and then that person gets to ask a friend for help. Even though there is no phone.

We miss the way you give us secret smiles that make us know you like us.

Not just some of us. All of us. You're fair. Also, you let us have fun, but if anybody gets carried away, you just give one of your looks.

We miss how you do the best voices when you read stories. You make the funny voices so hilarious we almost fall off our chairs and you make the scary voices so scary that Isabella covers up her ears. But not all the way because she still wants to hear you.

We are afraid for baby Ryan and for you. We can't get those tiny lungs out of our minds. We picture you holding Ryan's little hand. We hope you are not crying too much, but we think you might be.

We wrote a story for Ryan. Mr. Pinkerton even gave us time during class. We won him over with our charm.

We revised the story. Every sentence. We put our hearts and souls into it. We are keeping the passion burning.

Please read the story to baby Ryan. Do all the voices. Mali Koam said stories are like oxygen. We hope our story gives your baby a lot of good breaths. We hope our story gives him enough oxygen to last forever.

Love,
The Writers of Delite

Greetings, Mali Koam,

We did what you said and wrote an "I'm sorry" letter that worked like magic on Mr. Pinkerton. We also wrote an outrageously fantastic story for our teacher and her baby Ryan. We're sending you a copy. We hope the story makes the baby feel better.

Your fellow word-loving friends,

The Writers of Delite

P.S. Alas, we have the dreaded state tests next week, so we can't write any WOW stories during school. But we will keep writing.

Heart-Pounding News

by Kristin

After lunch today, Ms. Yang came into our room.

"I have some news for you," she said.

We thought it would be about the state tests. We had just finished taking them.

"It's about Ryan . . ."

You could hear the clock tick.

She gave us a letter from Mrs. Penrose.

Dear Friends,

I'm so sorry I couldn't write earlier. Ryan has needed all my attention.

Your card and your story made me laugh and cry. Happy tears, not sad ones. It was not only a beautiful gift, but also beautiful writing. I read the story to Ryan. I did all of the voices.

When I got to the part about the huddle, I missed all of you so much. You are the best students any teacher could ever want.

Ryan's brown eyes were open very wide during the story. I don't know how much he understands because he is so little, but I believe the story did just what you wanted it to do. Each sentence was a breath of air.

I know how much you like hearing your favorite stories over and over, so I will read this story to Ryan again and again. I'm sure it will become his favorite story. It is already mine.

Ryan is getting better every day. His lungs are growing. I know that you want me to come back, and I want to come back, too. But right now, Ryan still needs more of me. I hope you will understand. I will come for a visit as soon as I can.

Your teacher and greatest fan,
Mrs. Penrose

Dear Ryan,

You have a great mom. We can't wait to meet you.

Love, Jazmine and Tee

Dear Ry-Guy, keep growing. Don't forget to change your diaper. Ha-ha. Here's a poem for you:

> Roses are red
> Raindrops are plinky
> I bet you are cute
> even when you are stinky.

Smell ya later
(but you have to change your diaper first),
Nick

Greetings Ryan,

I am happy you are getting stronger. I plan on sending you some more stories and drawings. I will try not to make them too scary, but I must warn you that I am a big fan of suspense.

Fictionally yours,
Alexander

Dear Ryan (and Mrs. Penrose),

I'm glad you liked our story. I'm even more glad that you are okay. Sometimes good things happen.

Yours truly,
Isabella

Ryan,

Did you like my parts? Here is my advice. Whatever you do, don't give up. Mali Koam is right. I couldn't do a bicycle kick at first, but I have been practicing, and I finally did three in a row.

— Buzz

Hey Ryan (and Mrs. Penrose),

I knew you'd get better. I knew the story would be great. By the way, they announced the winner for that writing contest and it was a kid from Bettendorf, Iowa, not even anybody from Minnesota. I want to enter it next year. Can't wait to see you.

Your favorite student,
Carly

Dear Mrs. Penrose,

Thank you for writing back. We are all smiling here because:

1. Ryan is okay.

2. You're coming for a visit sometime.

Sincerely,
Omar

Dear Mrs. Penrose (and Ryan),

I thought the pins and needles were bad when we were waiting for advice from Mali Koam. But that was nothing compared to when we were waiting to hear about baby Ryan. We can't wait to see both of you.

—Kristen

Dear Ryan,

I just want to tell you something for when you are bigger. Here it is. If you ever have to move, you might be really scared and sad and even mad about it. But little by little it gets better. It's like you being in the hospital. Sometimes, it just takes time, and then it turns out okay.

Your new friend,

Harrison

A letter from our favorite author came!

— FROM THE DESK OF MALI KOAM —

Dear Writers,

Your story was brilliant. I was completely hooked. As Omar would say, I give it an A+.

Thank you so much for sharing it with me. I'm so pleased that you are using the power of words in such positive ways.

I have also written a letter to Mrs. Penrose, asking her to keep me posted on how things are going with the baby.

Here in Maryland, the snow has melted. I'm taking lots of walks with my writer's notebook. Today I saw purple flowers called crocuses. Spring has sprung.

Yours,
Mali Koam

Dear Mali Koam,

I used to say who would want to be a writer? Now I get it.

During spring break, I'm going to write a story about a soccer ball that wants to be kicked. The obstacle will be that it is stuck in a tree. It'll be a WOW story. I'm not going to tell you the end because it's so good you'll have to read it for yourself.

I also read "Fur" and "Secret Pages." They were the first books I read that I didn't have to read. There was only one problem. When I was reading "Secret Pages" I got in trouble because I was supposed to be doing my math. I love math, so that shows you how good your books are.

I just wanted to say thank you for the inspiration. And Carly says don't worry about not being rich. We are going to tell everybody to buy your books. It's spring break soon. Happy spring!

Your fan,
Buzz Benson

Harrison here. We only have many blank pages left in this book! Once it's done, let's keep it in the Good Book Nook so we can read it over and over.

Let's decorate the cover and think of a title!

—Jazmine

Dear Class,

What about creating a special place in the Good Book Nook now where you can put all your **WOW** stories? It will be like your own library of **WOW** stories. Students can check out a book by anybody and read it.

Sincerely,
Mr. Pinkerton

Yes! Alexander and Nick and I are going to write one together this week.

—Harrison

Dear Class,

    I have been pleased with your progress. I hope you all enjoy a wonderful spring break. I will see you all on Tuesday, April 1.

Sincerely,

Mr. Pinkerton

Back from Spring Break

A True Story by Buzz Benson

Nick was dying to make everyone laugh because it was April Fools' Day.

Unfortunately for him, we had a lot of work to do.

After many minutes of writing, Nick groaned.

"Ouch," he said. "I'm writing so much my fingers are going to fall off. Oh no!" Then he groaned again and there was a <u>clunk clunk clunk clunk</u> on the floor.

Isabella screamed because there were four fingers by Nick's desk!

"April Fools'," Nick said. They were fake fingers.

Everybody was laughing until Mr. Pinkerton stood up. He looked angry, and we all got very quiet. He walked over and picked up the fingers from the floor. "Nick, you are expelled from school," he said. "I'm calling your parents immediately." Then he stuck two of the fingers in his ears and said, "April Fools.' "

Hilarious!

— Buzz

LOL—Carly

WOW books are popping up in our room like spring flowers.

Over spring break, I wrote three WOW books. Jazmine, Harrison, Alexander and Buzz all wrote stories, too. Kristin and Isabella live near each other so they wrote one together. The big surprise is that Mr. Pinkerton wrote one, too. His is about a substitute who wants to do a good job, but the place that hires him is actually a zoo, and all of his students are actually monkeys. It's actually funny.

—Tee

Hey Everybody,

Omar, Nick and I are writing one together, too. It's a thriller. It's about two brilliant museum owners (a boy and a girl) who want people to come to their state flag museum, but the obstacle is a robber who steals all the flags, and they have to get them back.

The story is going to be suspenseful and funny. But that's not all! We want to make the museum for real. Only $1.00 to see all the flags. But you can check out our book from the Good Book Nook shelf for free, of course.

Carly

Dear Class,

Mr. Pinkerton showed me your WOW books. I am amazed and delighted. I'd like your permission to create a WOW shelf in the school library. I'd like to put copies of your books there and encourage all the students in the school to check them out. I'd also like to make copies of this very book and keep them in the library for students to check out, too, once you're done with it. I think you will inspire many other students and teachers to write stories of their own. May I have your permission?

Your librarian,
Ms. Yang

Hey,

It's exciting that Ms. Yang wants to put our WOW stories and this book in the library, but then everybody will know the secret of writing WOW stories. Next year, it will be even harder to win the contest. What do you guys think?

—Carly

Dear Carly,

Mali Koam shared her tips with us. I think we should share them with everybody. It will just mean there are more good stories in the world, which will mean we have to keep improving as writers. I think that's a good thing. Also, we might never win a contest, but if we let Ms. Yang put our books in the library, at least we'll be famous here at school!

—Harrison

Should We Give Permission for Our Books to Go in the Real Library?

Name	Yes or No?
Omar	Yes.
Isabella	Yes. Thank you.
Nick	Abso-dabbo-riggy-lutely.
Carly	Okay!
Kristin	Yes. I hope she puts real bar codes on them.
Alexander	Of course! I think Ms. Yang is going to need way more than one shelf.
Buzz	Yep. Hey, Alexander, will you add pictures to my soccer book?
Jazmine	Hurray!!!!!!!!!!!!!!!!!!!!
Harrison	This is a dream come true. I've always wanted to be an author.
Tee	Me too. (That is a yes.)

Ms. Yang made a WOW shelf in the library today, and she brought a letter from the office for Buzz!

— FROM THE DESK OF MALI KOAM —

Dear Buzz,

Thank you for your letter. I am so happy that you have grown to enjoy reading and writing. Have fun with your story about the soccer ball. Sounds like a winner.

Mrs. Penrose, Mr. Pinkerton, Ms. Yang and I have a surprise for your class. What is it? You'll have to wait to find out.

Suspensefully yours,

Mali Koam

Nick the Slick's Graphic Organizer

How Will Mrs. Penrose, Mr. Pinkerton, Ms. Yang and Mali Koam Surprise Us?

1. They'll tell us they're all vampires. Mwa-ha-ha.

2. They'll tell us that they're writing a book about us because they think we're vampires.

3. They got the state tests results and found out that we are all geniuses and we don't have to go to school anymore.

Guess who again. Before you get mad, here is the truth. Alexander gave me permission to write in here. Anyway, our class saw all your WOW stories in the library. I checked out three, and—I hate to admit it—they were fantastic. Now our class is writing some to put in the library. I was very depressed not to win that contest, but now I am excited to have this new project.

I'm sorry that I stole this book twice before, but I'm also kind of not sorry, because I really like this book and it's fun that I'm in it!

— Marcos

Thanks for sharing your tips. You guys are writing fun books. Please check out our books, too!

— DeeNice and Lauren

The Final Surprise

It was an ordinary day at Delite Elementary School. Outside, the smell of spring flowers floated up from the field next to the creek. Inside, the smell of breakfast sausages floated up from the cafeteria. The students and their teacher, Mr. Pinkerton, had just begun their lesson on writing.

"Today we're going to take a closer look at a literary device called a cliff-hanger," Mr. Pinkerton said. "Who can define the word 'cliff-hanger'?"

Nick jumped up on his chair, reached up to hold on to an imaginary cliff, and looked down at the floor with an expression of terror on his face.

Mr. Pinkerton laughed. "Okay. Nick is hanging from a cliff. Thank you, Nick. Is that what it means? Is a cliff-hanger someone who's in danger of falling to his doom?"

Kristin raised her hand.

"What do you think, Kristin?" Mr. Pinkerton asked.

"Well, I think—" Kristin said, and then the

classroom door opened with a <u>whoosh</u>.

Every head in the room turned to look.

Standing in the frame of the doorway was . . .

To be continued!

Just kidding.

It was Mrs. Penrose!

"Hi, friends," she said.

We jumped and cheered and basically went wild.

"Baby Ryan is still too small to come to school, but I have pictures!" she said, and pulled out her phone.

We gathered around her to look. He has fuzzy hair and big eyes. In one picture he's making a hilarious yawn that takes up his whole face. I mean, you could fit a whole piece of chocolate cake in there. In another picture he's wearing a white hat with bunny ears, which made us all say "Riggy!" In another picture you can see his fingers and his toes. Ten of everything. Perfect.

"Mrs. Penrose, I'm sorry," Mr. Pinkerton said, "but you'll have to leave. I was just about to give an important test."

Our eyeballs almost popped out of our faces we were so mad, and then Mr. Pinkerton said, "Just kidding."

Ha ha ha ha ha!

The dude has learned how to crack a joke. Actually, I think he picked it up from me, Nick the Slick, thank you very much.

"Can we take Mrs. Penrose to the library and show her our WOW stories?" Tee asked.

"Fine idea," he said.

~~We threw our papers and pencils into the air, yelled YIPPIE-AI-AYE at the top of our lungs, and ran out of the room.~~ We left our papers and pencils on our desks and walked to the library.

When Ms. Yang saw her old friend, she was thrilled. They hugged and Ms. Yang oohed and aahed over the pictures of baby Ryan just like we did.

"Your students have been working hard," Ms. Yang said. "Right, guys?"

We pulled Mrs. Penrose to a shelf that has a colorful label on it (which Alexander made) that says "WOW Stories."

Mrs. Penrose stood there with a look of deep appreciation on her face. A whole row of our books was there, waiting for their next readers.

"We have even more books than that," I said. "But people keep checking them out."

Mrs. Penrose pulled out a book. "'The Duck Who Wanted a Motorcycle'!" She laughed. She pulled out another. "'The Lonely French Fry'!" She pulled out another. "'Zombies on Ice'!" One by one, she read the title of each book. "I want to read them all."

"This is the one I wrote," Mr. Pinkerton said, and he showed her his story about the monkeys.

"I was inspired, too, and I collaborated with Alexander," Ms. Yang said. "Right, Alexander? We wrote one called 'Ghost in the Library,' and Alexander drew the pictures."

Alexander tried to find it, but it was checked out.

"Wow, wow, wow." Mrs. Penrose kept shaking her head like it was too good to be true.

"Speaking of WOW," Mr. Pinkerton said, "it is one minute before ten o'clock."

"Oh!" Ms. Yang jumped. "We have to get moving."

"What's going on?" Carly asked.

Mrs. Penrose gave us a big smile.

"Everybody to the rug by the smartboard," Ms. Yang said.

Once we were sitting down, she made us close our eyes. We heard a sound like a beep, beep, beep, beep from a telephone. Then we heard an unfamiliar voice.

"Hello, writers!"

We opened our eyes.

Skype was up on the smartboard, and a woman with glasses and a pencil stuck behind her ear was smiling and waving at us on the screen. She was sitting in a room full of sunlight with a cup of tea in one hand and a notebook on her desk. Behind her was a shelf full of books.

It was like the room was buzzing with incredible excitement even though we weren't moving. It was because we knew who she was, and we couldn't believe it.

"Harrison!" Alexander whispered. "It's her."

Mali Koam. We recognized her from the picture on her books. Mali Koam, sitting at her desk in Maryland, looking right at us.

"Hello, teachers. Hello, Writers of Delite," she said. "So nice to finally see you."

"Mali Koam!" Carly yelled. We all started waving and saying hello back.

"Salutations! What a beautiful library," she said.

Mr. Pinkerton pointed to the shelf behind us. "Those are just some of the WOW stories that you helped to inspire."

She got this look on her face, and she said, "You have no idea how happy that makes me."

And it hit me. First an author makes people happy by writing a great book, and then readers make the author happy by wanting to share it. If some of those readers write their own stories, the happiness just keeps growing.

"Mrs. Penrose, how is the baby?" she asked.

Mrs. Penrose held baby Ryan's picture up to the camera so she could see him.

"Aw," Mali Koam said. "What a cute little bunny-buddy."

That made everybody laugh.

"Seriously," Mrs. Penrose said. "Here's our chance to ask a real live author some questions. What questions do you have, class?" Harrison raised his hand. He got to stand by the camera.

"Do you ever feel like giving up?" Harrison asked.

"Writing is hard," Mali Koam said. "But letters from readers like you keep me going."

"Are you working on a new book right now?" Omar asked.

"I am." She held up a notebook and showed us her handwriting. It looked very messy. Omar was shocked.

Isabella got to go up and ask a question. "Have all your books been published?" she asked.

"No," she said. "I've written many books that didn't turn out good enough to publish. It's just like an athlete. You wouldn't expect a baseball player to hit a home run every time he or she steps up to the plate. Sometimes I strike out. But I keep trying."

You can guess who liked that part.

She read the first page of her new book, but she told us to keep it a secret, so I'm not going to write what it's about.

"We can't wait to read it," I said.

"No. We really can't wait," Alexander said. "So can you please do it as fast as possible?"

She laughed. "Yikes! A deadline! The pressure!"

"Will you put us in the story?" Carly asked.

She smiled. "You never know."

We had to say thank you and good-bye on the count of one, two, three. Good-bye, Mali Koam! And then she poofed off the screen. It was like magic.

A few minutes after that, we walked back to our classroom and then it was time for Mrs. Penrose to go. We were so sad.

Carly gave two friendships bands to her. One for her and one for Ryan.

Alexander got this book. "The pages are almost

completely full," he said. "Please, please write one last thing in it before you go. Then Ms. Yang is going to put it in the library."

"I'd love to," she said. "Also, baby Ryan sent something he wants to put in the book."

We were all curious.

Turn the page to see!

My Dear Writers of Delite,

Ryan loves your writing. So do I.

Your teacher,
Mrs. Penrose

If Ryan gets famous, I'm going to sell that footprint for a million bucks!

The End. Not.

ONE LAST DROP

* * *

Our pens are running out of ink.

Soon they'll go <u>kerplunk</u>!

Our brains need naps 'cause they've been goin'

think, think, thunk!

Our fingers are exhausted, too.

They need to stretch and bend.

Peace out. So long. Ta-ta for now.

This really is . . .

The End.

FOR THE STUDENTS AND STAFF AT RED ROCK ELEMENTARY SCHOOL IN WOODBURY, MINNESOTA. THEIR ENTHUSIASM FOR MY BOOK "PLEASE WRITE IN THIS BOOK" DURING OUR ANNUAL SKYPES AND THEIR AMAZING FOLLOW-UP LETTERS INSPIRED THIS STORY.

THANKS TO RED ROCK MEDIA SPECIALIST CARLA LARSEN AND TEACHERS LAURA LOPPNOW, TAMMY YOURCZEK, MICHELLE NELSON, JOAN HOLPER, SHANNA MILLER AND JULIANNE MOORE. I'M ALSO GRATEFUL TO NINA SCOTT, CLAIRE BULLOCK, THE HILARIOUS ETHAN LONG FOR HIS ILLUSTRATIONS AND MY EDITOR, MARY CASH, FOR GUIDING AND INSPIRING THE REVISIONS.

Library of Congress Cataloging-in-Publication Data
Amato, Mary.
Our teacher is a vampire and other (not) true stories / Mary Amato. — First edition.
pages cm
Summary: A notebook that is passed from student to student around a classroom becomes a repository for wild rumors, heartfelt confessions, and creative writing and helps the students cope when their teacher has a medical emergency and they must cope with a rigid substitute as they worry about their beloved teacher and her family.
ISBN 978-0-8234-3553-1 (hardcover)
[1. Teachers—Fiction. 2. Schools—Fiction. 3. Notebooks—Fiction.] I. Title.
PZ7.A49165Ou 2016
[Fic]—dc23
2015016726